PROMISCUOUS DREAMS©

THE THIRD NOVEL
of the
SECRET BUTTERFLY SERIES™

A NOVEL BY

Rosemary Lightfoot Ness-Bitner

A caution and disclaimer

All characters, events, and conversations in this book are fictional, the product of the author's imagination, or used fictitiously. Any resemblance to actual characters, living or dead, events past or present, localities, or conversations, is entirely coincidental.

If you are offended or stressed by characters' offensive behaviors and expressions of strong opinions about controversial subjects, you are advised and cautioned to not purchase this book or listen to this audio book. If you are a child under the age of eighteen, do not purchase this book or listen to this audio book as it contains erotic adult content. Sexual activity may cause diseases.

THIS BOOK CONTAINS SADISM, MURDER, AND EXPLICIT EROTIC ROMANCE CONTENT. IT IS INTENDED FOR MATURE READERS AND AUDIENCES OVER THE AGE OF EIGHTEEN ONLY. IT MAY BE OFFENSIVE OR STRESSFUL TO SOME READERS. OPINIONS, VIEWS, AND ADVICE GIVEN IN THIS BOOK BY ITS CHARACTERS TO OTHER CHARACTERS, AND BEHAVIORS EXHIBITED AND ADVOCATED BY ITS CHARACTERS DO NOT REFLECT THE OPINIONS, VIEWS, OR ADVICE, OR ADVOCATION OF BEHAVIORS OF, OR BY, THE AUTHOR OR PUBLISHER, OR OF, OR BY, ANY ORGANIZATION OR ENTITY TO WHICH THE AUTHOR OR PUBLISHER ARE AFFILIATED. NEITHER THE AUTHOR, THE PUBLISHER, NOR ANY OTHER PERSONS ASSOCIATED WITH THIS BOOK SHALL BE HELD RESPONSIBLE FOR ANY CONSEQUENCES ARISING FROM THE OPINIONS, VIEWS, ADVICES, BEHAVIORS, OR INTERPRETATIONS EXPRESSED BY THE CHARACTERS IN THIS BOOK; OR, IN ANY OTHER WAY, EXPRESSED IN THIS BOOK, OR BY ITS COVER.

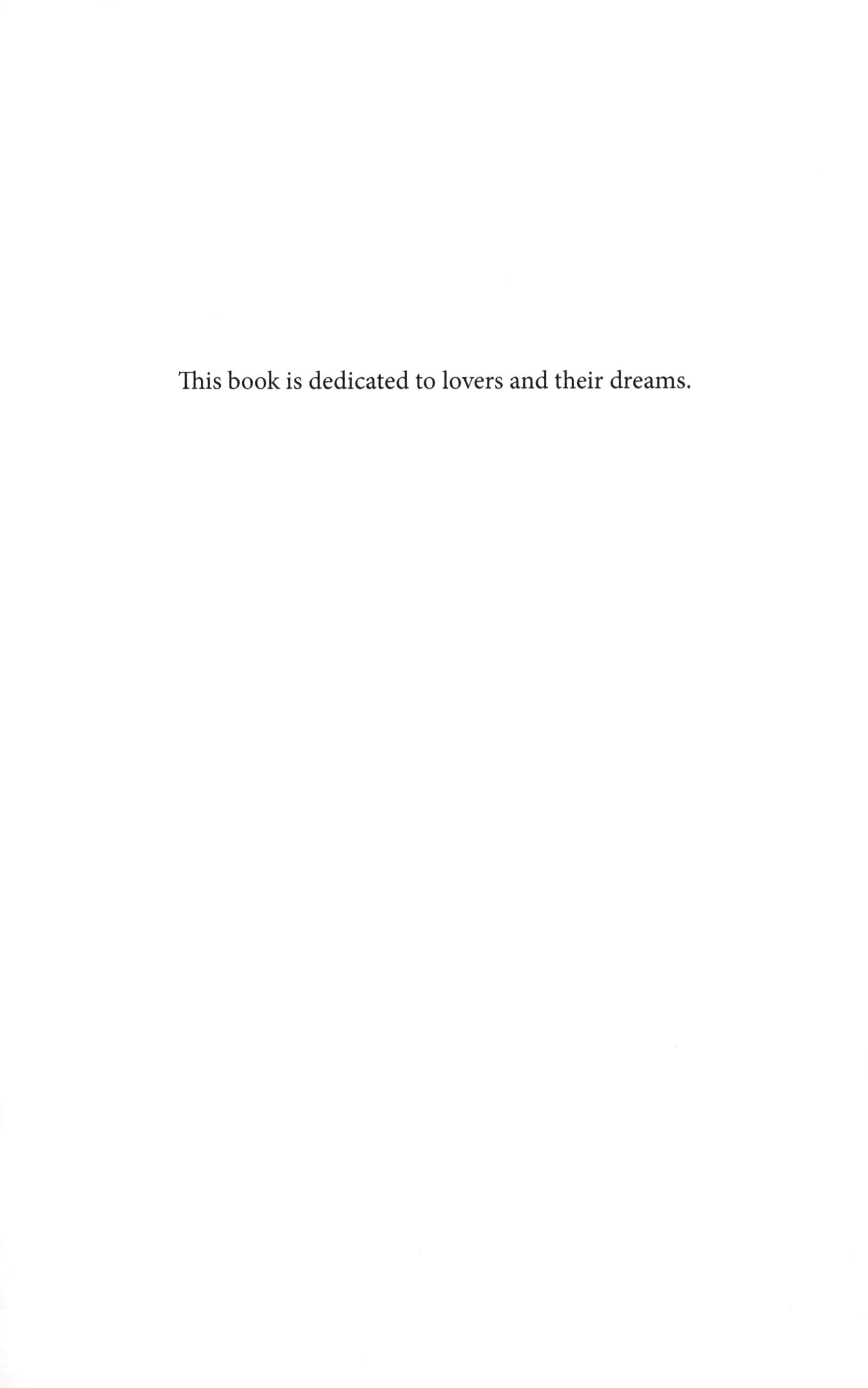

This book is dedicated to lovers and their dreams.

The eBook and print version layouts of PROMISCUOUS DREAMS were done by Andrea Reider. The cover was created by Cheeky Covers; and I am Melanie Monarch, your audio book narrator.

Hello dear listeners. This is Melanie Monarch, your audio narrator, bringing you PROMISCUOUS DREAMS, our third book of THE SECRET BUTTERFLY (tm) SERIES. What would you do if you suddenly discovered you had the world eating out of your hand, as Marty does? What might be going through our nymphomaniac's mind as she tries to sort out her choices and make decisions about her future? Will David want Marty in the company after hearing about her escapades and learning of her trusting liaison with Bertie and George? Notice how David probes her to understand her thoughts. Is he doing that because he loves her promiscuous ways? Is he thinking of ways to help her make her murders more pleasing? Could he, perhaps, be asking his questions for a hidden reason? Does David see himself as a CEO, or more as the secretive maestro of dysfunctional personalities? Yes, our David is a complicated fellow. Don't ignore anything he says or does, and don't let him out of your sight!

SECRET BUTTERFLY SERIES ™ CHARACTERS INTRODUCED IN "PROMISCUOUS DREAMS" (MAJOR CHARACTERS ARE BOLDFACED)

Readers reference guide to where a character is introduced.

(CHARACTER, DESCRIPTION OF CHARACTER, AND CHAPTER WHERE CHARACTER IS MENTIONED)

ASTARTE, MARTY'S REINCARNATION, TEMPLE PROSTITUTE, ENSLAVER, PIONEER OF FEMALE SEXUALITY AND BIRTH CONTROL, PROMISCUOUS DREAMS (PD), CH1

ANON, ADONAI, SON OF ASTARTE, (PD) CH1

BAAL, PRINCE OF DARKNESS, (PD) CH1

ISHTARA, MARTY'S REINCARNATION, MURDERESS, PERFORMER OF SACRIFICIAL RITUALS, ORGIES, (PD) CH1

BATHSHEBA, MARTY'S REINCARNATION, TEMPTRESS, MURDERESS, WIFE OF KING DAVID (PD) CH1

HANNA NOGA, FIRST WIFE OF KING DAVID, POISONED BY BATHSHEBA, (PD) CH1

SALOME, MARTY'S REINCARNATION, EXOTIC PAGAN EROTICIST, CONSORT, MURDERESS, (PD) CH1

CLEOPATRA, MARTY'S REINCARNATION, PTOLOMY QUEEN OF EGYPT, MURDERESS, SEDUCTRESS OF CEASAR AND MARK ANTHONY, (PD) CH1

ISABELLA, MARTY'S REINCARNATION, QUEEN OF SPAIN, PLUNDERER OF THE AMERICAS, INQUISITOR, MURDERESS OF MILLIONS, (PD) CH1

FERDINAND, POPE BORGIA (PIOUS THE SIXTH), CHRISTOPHER COLUMBUS, LOVERS OF QUEEN ISABELLA, (PD) CH1

GOSSIPS; EVELYN, MARJORIE, MARY LOU, SHARON, MARSHA, BECKY, MILLIE, JANE, PHIL, (PD), CH3

WINDHAM, BURNETT, JOHNSON, JOHN, REVELERS CHARMED BY MARTY, (PD), CH3

BIG ED, BILLIONAIRRE HUNTER, MARTY'S LOVER, SPONSOR, (PD), CH3

RITA, ORGY ENTHUSIAST, MARTY'S FRIEND, (PD), CH4

AMANDA, BERTIE'S DAUGHTER, OLYMPIC FIGURE SKATER, (PD), CH6

JOSH, THRILL SEEEKER, MARTY'S PREFERRED PORN PERFORMER, (PD), CH 6

CHAPTER ONE

Disease and depression concocted their brew. Famine and death did boldly ensue. Scattering, tattering families, those evil winds blew; while lust's desires grew, and grew, and grew, and grew. (Rosemary Ness-Bitner)

Good Hunting! (Rudyard Kipling: The Jungle Book)

CHANGING TIMES

It happened suddenly. Like a used rubber band, stretched too often and once too far, it snapped. The long overdue became due. Some said it happened because the ballooning debt bubble found a pin to prick it. Others said political rancor hardened positions and pulled consensus further apart, until there could no longer be consensus. Still others said it happened because their god had failed them. Astute observers first noticed the behavioral changes. House flipping no longer worked. The buyer at a higher price stopped buying. The jet skis, boats, campers, and vacation homes got thrown onto the markets. People needed cash. Rental house bookings fell, cancellations rose. Quietly, more changes took place. Reducing monthly maintenance costs, swimming pools were filled with dirt. Outdoor picnics in city parks replaced extravagant trips to far away places. Kids wore hand me down clothes. Times changed.

Government economists, central bankers and private sector economists produced reports. They assured people that price rises were temporary and transitory. Directors of central banks and big banks and little banks joined fellow board members giving speeches, assuring the public that things would soon return to normal; that everything was under control. But nothing was normal; normal was gone. People heard the speeches. They wanted to believe what they heard. They wanted to believe that their President was a man of integrity, committed to honorable service; not some angry, American hating, demented, low life, lying dirt bag grifter. People lived in a perpetual Halloween-like terror state, afraid to open secret closet doors and discover hidden skeletons of horrible treason-truths. They misplaced trust in sinister leaders who feasted on the carcass of a once great republic while selling them up the river. People were restless. Every time they went to the gas station or grocery store, they noticed that prices continued rising. They felt uneasy. They remembered. Gasoline and bread, not so long ago, cost less than half as much. What was the real reason for the changing prices? They wondered. Their gut told them they'd been lied to. They began questioning whether their banker-rulers and political leaders were delusional. Some had the temerity to openly criticized their leaders. This was their twilight dawning; their early penumbra time. Eyes and minds were opening to daylight's truths. Trust began slipping away. Yet, many still slumbered, believing that all was well; or hoping it would be. And a few prescient souls, like our clairvoyant Marty, had awakened before the crack of this new immoral dawning. They were already busily making the most of it.

Something weird was happening under the Earth's crust, too. Outside of Plaintown a hole opened in the ground and steam vented out of it. At first, people thought this was only a freakish curiosity. Children sat next to the hole and roasted hot dogs and marshmallows in the steam. Parents thought it was cute and harmless, until one morning. That was when a little girl picked up a dead bird near the hole and took it to her dad. Her dad came to the hole and stood by it. He listened carefully. He heard occasional deep gurgling noises that sounded ominous. Then a man from the government came with instruments to measure the gasses that came from the hole. The government soon issued a report. It reassured everyone that everything was perfectly safe and normal. But the report also told children to stay away from the hole. Alarmists said that Yellowstone was in early phases of a super volcanic eruption. The government's scientists disagreed. They said it was a natural occurrence that would soon go away. People believed the government. People always want to believe their government. Yet there was a sense of unease underlying everyone's behaviors. People suspected the hole. Some said it had opened for a reason.

Everything suddenly seemed uncertain. Nothing worked smoothly as they once did. Flights were often delayed or cancelled. Deliveries took too long. Mail delivery was unreliable. Spamming and fraud became the new normal. Political ideologies hardened. Opinions became rigid. People bickered. Compromise was scarce. Society bifurcated into peoples that were Haves and peoples that were Have-nots. The Haves had wealth and money. They could weather an economic storm. They could move far from the troublesome hole if the data from the hole worsened. Some didn't wait for more data. They moved. But the Have-nots didn't have the means to weather an economic storm. And they couldn't afford to move away from the hole.

Into the Have-not's camp tumbled the poor, the widowed, the orphaned and abandoned, the destitute and the homeless. Their social programs buckled and collapsed. Neighbor turned against neighbor, brother against brother, and sons against fathers. Mobs and vandals ruled city streets. Many people hit bottom. Children went hungry. New diseases appeared and progressed untended. Have-nots had no money for food or doctors. Despite bankers' assurances, banks failed. Goods became scarce. The stable, predictable world everyone once knew became unrecognizable. The American Dream was dying. Death was taking its place. And grave diggers were busy.

The smug and powerful Haves were aloof from plights of the poor. They pursued their quest for greater wealth and influence. They easily afforded food, shelter, and medicines to treat the new pathogens. A few tossed charitable guilt crumbs to the unfortunate poor. But mainly, these wealthy pursued their pleasures with carefree abandon. They wallowed in their luxuries while poor people suffered and died.

The advancing depression fostered extreme behaviors and polarized morals. The wealthy tightened their purse strings. Charitable giving slowed to a trickle. Corporations tightened their security. Merchants guarded their merchandise and boarded their storefronts. Businesses became less friendly. Foot traffic became adversarial. Many Haves felt fear. They stopped trusting and hardened their hearts. They withdrew; then became calloused; then became perversely amused about the unfortunate happenstances of the Have-nots. They hardened themselves against humanity's plight, sensing the world that had once been was not returning. Class warfare flared. Vandalism, thefts, and street riots became commonplace.

'May the devil take the hindmost' and *'It's every man for himself'* and *'They're finally getting what they voted for'* became cachets that expressed the Haves' sentiments. Many Haves strongly believed in their own abilities. They had no wants for food or material goods. The two main reasons that people turn to God: to seek help and to give thanks, were notably absent from the Have group. Seeing Have-nots turn to God, many Haves assumed that associating

with God brought bad luck. They ran away from God. Religious worship became stigmatized. Instead of seeking God, many Haves embraced sin.

At their dinner parties, the Haves compared fine wines and cuts of prime meats. They held grand galas and traveled, while the lifestyles of Have-nots fell further behind. While the Devil was having his due, taking the hindmost, the wealthy ignored the homeless, the starving, and the sick. They saw the pervasive homelessness. They heard the plights of the impoverished. But they reasoned that the problems were so overwhelming and so intractable that no solution was possible. So, they turned their backs on the despair of the unfortunate Have-nots. And they partied on.

Instead of embracing human sufferers, the Haves retreated into the psychological comforts of immediate self-gratification. Many Haves extolled the glories of debauchery and wickedness. They sought to outdo each other in their creative pursuits of pleasure. Civility's pretenses fell away. Perversities were condoned, even glorified. Sinfulness became socially approved. Evil doers went unpunished. Debauchery and corruption became widely accepted. Yesterday's gentility vanished. A sinister disdain toward the poor and unsuccessful took hold. Poverty, homelessness, and addiction were now viewed as the fault of the poor, the homeless, and the addicted. Times were changing.

This modern-day Haves' group resembled the depravity of the Roman Empire in its waning years. But modern society's downward spiral was still in its infancy. Innocents weren't crucified or torn apart by lions. Torture, quarterings and hangings were not public spectator sports. Those depraved horrors were reserved for the future. This was still that fabulously delicious penumbra transition time between the good times of the past and the difficult future times. During this frontier time, it paid handsomely to be a titillating fascination object of licentious pleasure seekers who could afford immorality's prices.

While families disintegrated and impoverished children starved and slept on sidewalks, wealthy men sought to escape the rising tide of social disintegration. A type of prestigious games-manship genre was born, which rapidly became the newest high society rage. Wealthy, image seeking men sought to enhance their social status by courting eye catching, trophy women. These men competed for the affections of notorious actresses, lav-ishing unimaginable riches upon them. Especially sought after were women who excelled in performing immoral erotica in the fast-growing adult film genre.

Studies in psychology and science encouraged a new, enlight-ened understanding of this newly reimagined, pornographic art venue. Society's new understanding galvanized around the gravitas of the human orgasm experience. The religious view that orgasm was sacrosanct, meant to be experienced only in the act of procre-ation, was displaced by a newer, laudable, amoral view of orgasm. This newer view gained rapid acceptance. It held that, through orgasm, men and women could unite in a psychological joining with their respective partners' souls; that once one had achieved this soul-sanctifying orgasm intimacy with another human, the effect of their limbic union was life-long lasting, possibly eternal; possibly binding enough to survive mortal death and these united souls' resurrections.

With this new view of the profound importance and immoral holiness of explicit, orgasm producing sex, pornography became more than respectable. It became venerated; desirable as an expansive, communicative, connecting art form to be appreciated, understood, and revered. With its new interpretation, people now raved over porn. Many termed it their 'gush,' their ultimate artis-tic medium which enabled them to feel connected to humanity's needs and progress. It became the ultimate mainstream art form which enabled its viewers to observe how these eternal, intimate liaisons; these profound unions of human feelings were often spontaneously created. Female porn stars who could elicit these expressive feelings; who could memorialize their limbic connections to their partners in their film craft, became the new maestros of this Avant Garde artistic expression.

Major colleges and universities scrambled to capture the exploding interest in the new social phenomenon. Curricula were expanded to include major studies programs in pornography. Course offerings included: Porn as Art; The history of Porn; Filming Porn; Penis and vagina positions for optimal coitus expression; Managing a Porn Star; Marketing Porn; Legal issues in Porn; Psychological aspects of Porn; Case studies of Porn Stars' lives; and audition techniques for aspiring Porn Stars. These course offerings were quickly oversubscribed. Tuition rates for the new courses commanded premium payment. Love and adoration of porn stars and their film works swept over academia, as it did over the general public. Wave after wave of new, titillating revelations about porn, its star performers, their affairs, and musings, enveloped a porn thirsting nation; each new wave featuring exciting new stars and breathtakingly new pornographic themes.

Porn stars became idolized. Their orgasms were studied and compared with those of other porn stars. How they responded to different partners; how they appeared to feel at different moments in their films, were all nuances that were scrutinized, discussed, and compared. Pictures of these women's expressions during their orgasms became desired, must have, items for millions of porn aficionados. These pictures, especially when autographed, became treasured items; traded with fervor. Prices of exceptional porn scene photos were bid up to astronomical levels; one such original, rare photo fetching over two million dollars. Collecting porn stars' photos became more crazed than baseball card and sports memorabilia. Understanding the female orgasm, in all its permutations and expressive forms, became America's new national obsession.

Demand for the erotic films of notorious porn stars skyrocketed. These women, who engendered feelings of adoration, love, and wonderment in the hearts and minds of their fans, were openly coveted by wealthy alpha males. Top social males no longer disguised their passion lusts. They flaunted them. Notorious, shameless porn stars were their honored guests at many social functions, often introduced by their hosts and hostesses and asked to stand and bow to the applause of audiences and dinner guests; and asked to give speeches upon receipt of awards and prizes for their profligate immorality. To be recognized as a profligate, notoriously famous porn star was to have arrived at the pinnacle of high society. Memberships in these porn stars' premium services burgeoned, despite ever increasing costs of membership.

Pornography became an upscale frenzy. Suddenly it was Avant Guard, exciting and new. It took everyone's mind off the dismal times. Both rich and poor empathized with these adorable nymphs. Many idolized and obsessed over them. Articles about their favorite fetishes, perversions, diets, sex routines, companion lovers; and especially their opinions about all sorts of otherwise banal issues, became topics of the collective mind. Entire articles were written and interviews conducted that delved into the most granular levels of these women's thoughts and feelings, especially as their thoughts were taking place while they were performing their explicit love scenes; and particularly what they thought about and how they felt while having their orgasms with different partners in different settings.

Many young women dreamed to enter this fantasy-like world. Stardom offered a young lady a way to escape from a society overextended by debts and besieged by intrusions into individual privacy. Sex instantly whisked away those stresses. Public attitudes about sex were rapidly changing. More and more, pornography and sex artistry took on many attributes of spectator sports. It was a refreshingly new entertainment venue; seen as beautiful, loving, magical; an acceptable alternative pursuit to violence and drudgery. Porn stars were chased by paparazzi for their photos and quotes. Fans hounded them for their autographs. In this new-normal orgasm-centric world, sex workers commanded elitist status, fame, notoriety, and a glamorous, upper crust cachet.

Pagan cults, with their historic roots in sex worship, suddenly experienced a revival from their millennial dormancy. In new Pagan temples of sin, worshiping members from both wealthy and poor freely mingled. A new phenomenon called the Modern Morality Standard swept the land. Sex and immorality became American culture's acceptable New Normal. Many people became sex obsessed. Sex addiction was widely acknowledged and treated by prescribing even more sex.

Minutia of erotic performances were carefully studied and compared. Magazines and televised talk shows compared the expressiveness of mouths and fingers during felatio; the relative merits of different explicit erotic scenes; the amatory credibility of various pornographic performers' facial expressions during their orgasms; etc. The Haves feasted on a diet of graphic, explicit print, audio, and visual debauchery in an endless smorgasbord of bountiful erotica. Demand for explicit intimacy art in all media formats seemed insatiable. Shameless uninhibited sex work became society's newest opportunity; a social ladder up for many women.

What were once shamed associations were suddenly in vogue. Having a beautiful sex goddess on one's arm became a dominant male's bold, brazen fashion statement. Only the wealthiest could afford the most sensuous, most titillating, and most sensationally immoral whores. Much like the debauched times of decadent Rome, these whores, particularly the most notorious porn stars, were given open access and residences in homes of wealthy men. These salacious women were fawned over and idolized. They achieved goddess status.

This was a time of great societal stress where immediacy and instant gratification were at the forefront of behaviors and decision making. Established values and norms became distrusted, viewed skeptically, often criticized, openly scorned; and then discarded for something that worked better.

'Why must I wait for my death to discover glory?' a man might ask himself. *'When my concubine slips her panties off, I can hold her in my arms, take her to my bed, and experience nirvana in the here and now,'* his reasoning went. Explosive mob rule lurked just below civilization's fragile façade, bubbling, and seething like a latent volcano. It had long wanted to throw over its long-trusted institutions and embrace lust and base behavior. And it had long waited patiently. It had waited for its opportunity to upend the social order and return humankind's morality to its more natural Pagan practices; knowing its day would come.

Attendance at traditional religious services plummeted while societal norms were being flipped upside down. Morality was subsumed in a sea of lasciviousness. Erotic film stars were highly compensated and idolized for the titillating explicit roles they played. Exploits of adult actresses were now closely followed and reported on, even by mainstream media venues as well as by gossip tabloids. An eager public devoured every scintillating tidbit about the lives of their favorite porn stars.

The more ribald; the more risqué and depraved these women's behaviors, the greater became their audience reach and popularity. Their admirers ogled their designer dresses; idolized the creative ways they revealed their heavenly cleavages, concavities, and derrieres. These purveyors of casual immorality became deified icons during this blossoming era of sin. Even the most devout, steadfastly religious leaders wondered whether God had failed them.

In these new, normal times, what more luxurious, rewarding, and honored positions could possibly be better than the life styles of these beautiful erotic film actresses? In what other professions or venues could a woman, unhindered by a moral compass, receive better treatment and compensation than by becoming a profligate, lavishly pampered, celebrated, notorious whore? What better time could there *be,* to be exalted and heralded for one's own sociopathy, than *this* time? What *better* time could there be, *to be Marty?*

DAYDREAMS

Marty was deep in thought about the day's earlier events. Like a successful snake that devoured a prey rabbit, she now digested how she destroyed her naive, witless competitor. She smiled, pleased knowing that she'd likely never see Carl's wife again. Her sense of invincibility occasioned her to stimulate herself while Carl slept.

Outside the cabin, high up in a pine bough, the Clark's Jay ruffled its feathers in anticipation of sleep. Somewhere from across the lake the cougar screamed its warning to a coyote that dared to approach its kill. A light breeze rustled the pines outside the cabin. Nature tried to lull Marty into slumber. Her body was exhausted from making love with Carl. But her mind wasn't ready to relax. She always imagined things forward. Her mind worked that way. It kept her thinking ahead, paying attention to details. She liked seeing herself in future situations, imagining what people would do and say; imagining her initiation of it all; then imagining her responses to peoples' reactions. Her mind was always a restless place.

Even while Marty slept, she had vivid dreams, filled with interactions with people. And, the personalities of her inner voices, their instructions, and their opinions readily integrated themselves into these dreams. Her voices always intertwined themselves with her thoughts. Tonight, she was trying to visualize the future before she let herself fall into her dreams. She closed her eyes and waited to hear from her voices.

They came soon enough. They were never far away. Now, entering her mind, they again engaged her thoughts. They understood that the day's conquests had not fully satisfied her nymphomania. Her clitoral nerves had already begun tingling in anticipation of Fred. Her legs signaled that they wanted him. She imagined feeling his body clasped tightly within her thighs. She smiled, anticipating the pleasures that lie ahead. Sex with Fred would be much better this time. He had told her he was eager to learn the things she wanted to teach him.

She became sleep aroused. Thoughts of Fred's money stimulated her. She had learned and confirmed on her first visit that he had wealth. Before, she could only guess, based on appearances. Now she knew that Fred had far more money than Carl would ever have. That thought made her loins throb more intensely. She wanted to convert his fortune to her own purposes. Her dreams became more real, more pleasing. She was imagining Fred had already entered her. That excited her. She stirred and moaned in her sleep. This dream felt good. She wanted more of Fred, and more of his money; and she knew she could have more of both. Her loins never lied.

'Look ahead, Marty,' whispered Miss Promiscuity. 'From now on, Carl will be easy for you. With his wife out of the way, you can have Carl whenever you want him; but Fred is a much bigger catch. He has all that MONEY, and he WANTS YOU! He's told you he's in

LOVE with you. Concentrate on what's important. I'm anxious to see how much fun we'll have.'

'Let's first ease his wife out of the picture,' said Miss Iniquity. *'She's a silly, hapless fool. She doesn't suspect anything. She doesn't even know we're playing the game we're playing. She'll be gone all weekend. It's your perfect chance to make your lasting impression on Fred. Test him. Push him along. See how far he's willing to go.'*

'Go with your gut instincts, girl,' giggled Miss Shameless. *'Remember when Miss Iniquity told you it was high risk to make that orgy film with six black partners; but I told you it felt right and natural; so, you embraced that opportunity and performed it? Remember how wonderful you felt, having sex all afternoon with those six handsome black men? Remember how highly stimulated you felt from all those black hands touching you everywhere, how you felt so titillated to be flaunting all the racial taboos?*

'That's when you melted Marshawn's heart. He confessed his love for you, Remember? When Aaliyah, his jealous wife, discovered that naughty gift you gave him, she launched herself into orbit around Pluto. How could you ever forget all the uproar she caused? Aaliyah created priceless publicity for you. I told you it would work out because we both knew it felt right, didn't I? Yes, you created something wonderful. We made our breakthrough into loving immorality when we made that film. We broke every racial barrier; and we did it so casually, so naturally. Remember how much we enjoyed it? You opened millions of minds to new discoveries; opened the door to possibilities of beauty and love; helped people see how glorious it was!

'Your immoral whoring suddenly became virtuous and celebrated by millions of new fans. You gained market share fast by listening to me. You encouraged those beautiful men to taste you, sup delicious nectars they had once thought were forbidden. Well, we changed all that, didn't we? The porn magazines portrayed you

as deliciously, sweetly innocent; doing your honest best to break down racial barriers. Your publicists, George, and Bertie, positioned you as the icon of humanity's inevitable progress. Now, whenever a woman performs with a black cock they are reminded of your spectacular film where, one huge black cock after the other, tapped its head against your outer lips, as if begging to enter you. And then, slowly, lovingly, and adoringly entering you.

'Your viewing fans could readily imagine how hot and juicy you were as those magnificent shafts probed deeper into you. They could only dream how wonderful those cocks felt as you twerked and yawed your vagina until they exploded their semen into you. They loved you in that film. Your fans imagined that they were holding you and kissing you while you fucked your partners; and they dreamed that, one day, they might luckily enter you as well. You are worshipped by millions now. You are immorality's goddess.

'You peeled away the fading veneer of false modesty and let the world share your liberating sexual glory. Someone had to do it first. You'll always be honored for that breakthrough film. That's how your life touches everyone, Marty. Your performances are innovating and transformative. Your fans love them. They idolize you. They salivate at the many ways you shatter social norms. Your films are triumphs of immoral splendor. You awakened the spirits of millions. Their spirits rise up at the thought of you. Their hearts cheered their newly felt freedoms. Your breathtaking explicit erotica opens their eyes to the highest heights of carnal bliss. You pave the way forward. Explicit love making has become the ultimate, nuevo art form. And your beautiful face expresses it all! Your joys have opened millions of minds! People embrace sexual possibilities they never imagined existed before.

'Some women of color are now calling you The Immoral White Nemesis. Do we really care? Their resentment is a blessing. It has spread your reputation for ravenous immorality even wider; and

that has opened a vast, new market for your artistry. You'll soon be creating three new films where you will partner with black lovers. You already know those films will be fabulously successful. Remember how you felt on that set? Those men gave you their honest love. And you responded beautifully. You know we can replicate that.

'Remember how you savored those explicit erotic moments? Remember all the semen cream flowing from their magnificent black cocks? Can't you still feel it streaming into you? Sure, you can. I can see you are dreaming about it. Your mind exploded with such insatiable lust that day. You wished those adoring cocks would continue spurting their creamy white into you, forever. You craved more and more of it! And when you sucked their cocks' heads afterwards and drew out still more semen, you felt liberated and gloriously beautiful, didn't you? You did, because you were!

'And you saw what that film did for your career! People downloaded hundreds of thousands of copies. You became celebrated and talked about as the most casually immoral whore in the world; and your porn ranking shot up from the middle thousand into the top twenty, didn't it? That's why we must create more films with handsome black partners and with new, creative themes.

'Now you have a premium service, with men calling you from all over the world, just begging to make love with you. Advertising buy-ins from prostitution services and cam girl providers are going through the roof. Hundreds of prostitutes, nationwide, signed contracts to piggy-back their services onto your films. Your EYES BEHIND THE BUTTERFLY ™ branded clothing and merchandise sales at your SECRETBUTTERFLYSERIES.STORE are doing extremely well. You get hundreds of letters from your devoted fans every single day; many sending you their favorite porn photo of you, begging you to autograph it and return it to them. Many now clip several hundred-dollar bills to their requests and professing that they adore you and want you to create more films.

'You recently released your 'DOING WHAT I LOVE' porn pictures photo album series. They are sensational sellers; especially your newest one with its full-sized layouts capturing wide angle explicit close ups of your beautiful face and mouth performing different phases of fellatio and vaginal fornication scenes with your favorite hundred penises. It's simply breathtaking. Your albums are finding their way onto hundreds of thousands of coffee tables in homes all over the world, further expanding the demand for more of every film you create.

'Your innovative marketing has opened the public's appetite for your pornography wider than it ever was before. You've breathed fresh life and acceptability into prostitution, Marty. You represent the cleansing release, that honest, refreshing, shameless wholesomeness and honest fun that glorious, unapologetic whoring brings to so many stressed out millions.

'You've advanced prostitution's acceptance as the legitimate alternative for thirsting souls who are drowning in traditional dogmas. Your fame is on a very fast growth curve. You know it's all true! That's because you listened to me, Miss Shameless. Remember what Mrs. O'Dell told you? She said prostitution and erotic films are the perfect career path for you. Look how well your courageous shamelessness and your Avant Garde films complement our immoral modern society!

'People are tired of corrupt politics and fake news. They don't want to think about that stuff or hear about it anymore. They want you, Marty. They want your honest immorality! They idolize you! Remember how Mrs. O'Dell told you to get a coach for those on-screen scenes; your make up, wardrobe; and yes, even your different fornication techniques? She told you if you stayed alert for opportunities and played your cards right you could easily become the world's number one erotic film actress. Well, she was right! And so am I!'

Unexpectedly and suddenly, Miss Iniquity's authoritarian voice spoke from a deeper part of Marty's slumbering brain. She always brought her voice into Marty's mind like that. It was her controlling way. It jolted Marty. She twitched in her sleep.

'I apologize. I was wrong to oppose creating the orgy film with the six blacks. I admit it.' Iniquity didn't make long fusses or excuses about her judgment misses. She just addressed them and moved on. She had a mysterious power that Marty's other voices didn't have. She didn't reveal her power often, but she decided that now was as good a time as any, maybe better. After all, despite her reserved pragmatism, she always sought to advance Marty's best interests.

'If you want to get to the top of your profession,' Iniquity's husky voice spoke in her half whisper, half forceful way which made sure her points were heard, *'then you need to understand the soul you carry around inside your body. It's the reincarnation soul of strong women who refused to be pushed around. They didn't accept second place. Like you, they were all stunning, beautiful women; and like you, they were all glorious whores; but unlike you, they never, in any way, tried to disguise who they were or what they were all about. Follow?'*

Marty shook her sleeping head ever so slightly. Her dreams had never delved into her soul's history before tonight.

'Okay,' whispered Miss Iniquity in her lowered voice tone, *'since you've declared where you intend to take your career, I'll give you the full reveal. I'll let you see into your soul, like the eyes of the Monarch butterfly can see. Once you understand your own soul, you can place yourself on top of the entire world. You alone have the power to do that.*

'You must be ruthless and willful, like your predecessors. I'll mention a few of the bodies that carried your soul throughout its history. You've possibly heard the sanitized versions of their lives, but

to appreciate their determination to succeed you must understand their true underlying characters. These were women who were all driven to succeed.

'Your first reincarnations were as Astarte, the high priestess temple whore of Baal who lived about nine thousand years ago; and later as her descendant, Ishtara. As Astarte you fornicated in religious solar rituals in the Temple of Baalbek, where you honored the solar cycle. You commanded all adult males in your tribe to come before you and the other temple prostitutes at every full moon to purify themselves from their evil thoughts and misdeeds; submitting to the mysteries of nature and renewal of life by entering your holy of holies between your legs and there fornicating with you and ejaculating their semen into your vaginas. You held special services to purify and sanctify conjugal unions of men and women; and to bless the fertility of the fields and the animals; and to allow for tribal members to atone to you for whatever transgressions they had committed. In this way you maintained a harmonious, ordered society.

'You convinced the twelve strongest clans in the Beqaa Valley to pledge loyalty under your yoke, by promising them food, peace, and prosperity if they worshipped you. You solidified your rule through your prostitution rituals and bonded those scattered clans into your unified tribe. You understood the solidifying magic of your breathtakingly beautiful ceremonies and your explicit pagan pornography. You performed explicit sexual acts of fornication and fellatio with your tribal leaders to bind their loyalties to you. You swallowed their semen, thus purifying them and taking into yourself their life essences and completely unifying their loyalties to you.

'You commanded that your followers build you the greatest temple in the world, complete with massive foundation stones and fornication altars to honor your temple whores' prostitution rituals during the phases of the solar cycle. Your followers first conquered the entire fertile Beqaa Valley; then the entire known world. All who

opposed your fornication rites and your requirements for their tribute tithes were put to the sword.

'You were the first woman to shave her vagina's mons, using an obsidian blade to make your pubic area smooth and appealing. That encouraged your men and women followers to lose their inhibitions and feel good and wholesome about performing cunnilingus with you. You were also the first woman to use perfumed aphrodisiacs and oils to make your vagina irresistible to males' worship lusts. You were the first woman to claim your rights to your own body; practicing birth control by placing strips of acacia leaves in your vagina to neutralize your male lovers' semen. You were the first woman to openly advocate and shamelessly champion the practice of ritual pornography. You fornicated with Baal, highlighting his splendid penis in eloquent, grand ceremonies before your adoring, lusting followers. Your pornographic deeds were praised and glorified as the newest, most beautiful, living art form. You became notorious. Your fame and adulation spread across the land. Many journeyed from afar to witness your performances. You were worshipped for your shameless, uninhibited debauchery; and your spectacular orgies. Your spectacularly ruthless murder sacrificing's of your enemies were breathtaking. You were cheered and applauded. The people sang songs of your praise. They flocked to your execution and massacre ceremonies to kiss your feet and bring you gifts of foods, precious jewels, skins, and furs.

'You commanded your tribesmen to conquer all other tribes for hundreds of miles in all directions. Your followers conquered the tribes of Gobekli Tepe. You had their largest temple dismantled and its massive stones placed upon wooden sleds; then dragged on skids southwest for 365 miles to Baalbek. There, the stones were reassembled to form the foundation of your magnificent temple of prostitution. You quarried additional stones from neighboring quarries and placed your own stones on top of your conquered peoples' stones.

Fittingly, you fornicated upon your altar, high above the conquered stones, for all glory of this great historic conquest was attributed to your leadership. You ordered your conquered tribes back to Gobekli Tepe. You forced those peoples to bury their old temples, destroying all traces of their civilization. Work done; you marched your captives back to Baalbek.

'You then had your victims tortured, enslaved, and murdered; their flesh rendered and fed to your followers; their bones ground to make mortar cement for your temple columns and fornication altars. You and your twelve tribal leaders held a blood feast. You shared the flesh of the conquered peoples' king and you drank his blood from a shared chalice. This ceremony solidified your power. It bonded the souls of your tribesmen to your soul. Your reign as queen of Baalbek taught your soul two valuable lessons. First, a strong woman needs to organize men and plan their actions and tell them what she wants done. Many reincarnations later this experience served you well, helping you organize your Private Member Services prostitution business. Secondly, you gained your profoundly important understanding of male lust. Your male worshippers suspended clan morality and vanquished an entire civilization to experience the glory of fornicating with you and worshipping your blood thirsty vagina. You learned that the promise of pleasures with you could incentivize men to inflict mortal harm upon others.

'With Baal, Prince of Darkness, you produced a son, Anon, who left the valley and expanded his name to Adonai. He declared himself God, and ordered all conquered desert peoples East of your valley to worship him; and later to call him their god, by his name Adonai. His name became legend. Thousands of years after his death, the Hebrew tribesman, Abraham, adopted Adonai as the name for his God.

'Millenniums later, as Ishtara, you murdered countless innocents. You stabbed them, threw them into the temple's sacrificial

fires; decapitated and impaled them; you did to them whatever pleased you and whatever enhanced your power in the eyes of your tribe. You ordered your tribal warriors to plunder, pillage and enslave neighboring tribes. You held sacrifices of the captives in honor of your fornications, thus sustaining the fertility of your conquered lands and the power of your tribe. Your fornication rituals explored the sensuous possibilities of fornication methods and tested the limits of promiscuity. You greatly expanded the practice of pornography in your religious ceremonies by introducing orgy rituals, and thereby introduced communal sexual freedom to humankind. To maintain your power, you required every member of your tribe to faithfully honor your prostitution rites by paying a tithe to you, without exception. When one man tried to deceive you and deny the payment of his rightful tithe, you had his daughter show him that only you decided the acceptable way to honor you. You showed him that his feeble attempt at male dominance would not be tolerated. You demonstrated, through your control of his daughter, that your vagina was the only true deity, remember?'

Marty nodded. From somewhere in the recesses of her memory, Iniquity's recounting of that event rang true. That daughter had murdered her father before Ishtara's approving eyes, thereby pleasing Ishtara and earning Ishtara's enduring love. Miss Iniquity then focused her reveal on Marty's next reincarnated soul, Bathsheba:

'Bathsheba was another body that hosted your soul. You arranged your husband's certain death so you could whore with King David. You were not about to let marriage or modesty prevent you from getting the number one place in the Hebrews' growing kingdom. You felt love and passion for King David. You knew those feelings were more sacred than your marriage to your husband. You sought to free yourself and the King from the inhibiting constraints of marriage and to purify each other in the splendor of passionate intimacy. You

weren't about to allow your own husband's yoke of marriage bully you. You refused to deny what your lusts told you was rightfully yours. You set up your husband's murder beautifully by seducing King David, remember?'

Again, Marty's memory was touched. She nodded.

'Then, you dispensed with Hanna Noga, Grace of Light, and King David's unrecorded first ranked wife, by cleverly poisoning her with your lamb stew offering of friendship, spiced with deadly oleander. The day after David ended his Shiva mourning for Noga, he married you. Your darkness swallowed her light. Your passions were finally sated. Your whoring placed you on the throne of Israel. Remember?

Marty smiled. Her soul remembered the rewards and pleasures of Bathsheba's relentless determination. She had eliminated her bullying husband and ensconced herself as Queen by her deliciously murderous whoring. Marty recognized this timeless pattern of iniquitous whoring. She knew her soul had inherited it, naturally. She understood Miss Iniquity's message: immorality in pursuit of a greater good for herself was noble and glorious; a behavior to be praised and honored; and never a reason for guilt or shame.

'Sometime later,' continued Miss Iniquity, *'your soul assumed the body of Salome. You loved combining your dancing with your whoring then, as you do now. When the Baptist prophet hurled insults your way, you didn't equivocate. You knew what to do with your detractors and enemies. You did not allow that self-righteous mad man to bully you with his insults; or to make you feel guilty about being the glorious, beautiful whore that you were. You were proud of who you were and what you did. You enlightened men's hearts; purified them from their inhibitions; and bound their loyalties to you and your king, by offering them your pleasures. Your patience with the mad man's disrespectful insults had finally expired. You chose to brook no more of his nonsensical gibberish.*

'Remember how you arranged to give the babbling madman his just deserts? You performed your private lap dance with the King. You French kissed him; and fondled and mouthed his balls; you kissed the head of his cock. You touched his cock's head to your vagina's outer lips, letting him feel your slippery heat, driving him nearly insane with lust. You gave him samples of the sensational fellatios he would receive, after he granted your request.

'That historic day you wore a sheer see-through silken-lace gown and matching silk slippers. Your enticing breasts were visible through your gown. Your nipples protruded noticeably. Your hair was perfectly coiffed. You wore gold bracelets, gold anklets and a pearl neckless. You were scented with verbena, gardenia, and lavender. Your lipstick was a delicious shade of deep red; your eyes were shaded with a soft taupe. When you entered the court, the invited guests gasped at your beauty. They were stunned; mesmerized. They admired you as you took your rightful seat at the right hand of the king. You staged your entrance brilliantly. You were confident, serene; knowing you deserved the King's payment offering. The lunatic Baptist was brought before you and made to kneel at your feet. You took your hand to his chin and lifted his head to behold you. Then, you opened your gown so he could behold your naked beauty. He stared, dumbstruck, into your vagina, knowing that he would never partake of its glorious pleasures. You told him to behold his true God, the God that held the power of life and death over him. You commanded him to kiss your vagina; and he turned his head away from you; defiling you. Then, you ordered him taken away and have his defiant head returned to you, without his body attached. The lunatic's stubborn, self-righteous head was then decapitated and returned to you; served up to you, upon a silver platter; so, it could be made to stare upon your triumphant vagina.

'You arose from your throne chair and descended the dais steps to the severed head. You let your gown fall to the floor; and you *stood naked before your detractor's head. You cupped your breasts before the head, mocking it; showing it the loveliness it would never know. Then you lifted the wretch's head and held his lips to your vagina's lips, further mocking him; showing the King and his court that you would not tolerate detractors or insulters. You smiled to the king, opened your arm to him, and invited him to come join you and share your gift. He arose, descended the steps, and came behind you. He placed one arm around your belly; and reached his hand lower, touching your vagina, stimulating you. He raised his other hand and cupped your breast. Then, you turned your head to his and kissed him full on the mouth with a tantalizing French kiss. You let the severed head fall to the palace floor, symbolizing its powerlessness, as you embraced the King.*

'Remember the king's words when he declared that your lips had silenced the lips of the heretic. He proclaimed that your lips were the only lips that showed the true path to glory and purity of salvation. He announced that your glorious immoral vagina was the only true god that he and his kingdom needed. He then took you to his private chambers. He immediately slid his face beneath your adorable, succulent vagina and performed delicious cunnilingus with you. He then ejaculated into your vagina; thus making himself pure and freeing you from any blood-guilt.

'Your victory was complete. You had murdered and defiled the lunatic who had tried to bully you. You demonstrated the nonsensical madness of his prophesies by rubbing his face in your vagina. His god did not come to rescue him or come to punish you. His god never challenged how glorious and shameless you were after you removed that obstinate, self-proclaimed prophet obstacle to your rightful status. Remember how liberated and marvelous you felt when your whoring could no longer be doubted as the kingdom's true religion?

'That event contrasted the difference between your honest immorality and his nonsensical blather spew about some

imaginary goodness. You symbolically let the king's court know you were fearless and shameless about your immorality. Rather, you proved that your whoring vagina was honest and healthy; goodly and pure for its honoring of life and creation's mysteries. The event was a historic first. You offered the kingdom's people a true choice. Did the people want to choose the traditional misogynistic religious way, where they worshipped, deified, and honored death; or did they prefer your Pagan ways of celebrating, worshipping, respecting, and honoring life and life's creation processes? You demonstrated that the honest immorality of your wanton vagina was more powerful. And it made common sense. And the blather spewer's imaginary, other worldly madness made no sense, except to lunatics. You copulated wantonly, openly, and freely with your king and kept your King true to his natural common sense. He appreciated you for showing him the righteously immoral path forward. He lavished gold and jewels upon you, glorifying your sensational whoring. And he exalted you; raising you up to sit on your throne chair, by his right hand; thereby honoring you as the most divine whore in his kingdom.

'News of your triumph spread. You became the most favored whore of all the visiting kings. They all offered you and the king exorbitant gifts to touch, kiss, fondle, and worship you, by fornicating openly and unashamedly with you, in your king's court. And they paid tribute to you and your king. And they concluded treaties with your kingdom by surrendering themselves to you in your bed, remember? You greatly advanced your power and the king's power with your magnificent, glorious, shameless whoring. And your king appreciated you. He praised you and loved you and adored you.

'There are times when a woman must assert herself and not allow herself to be bullied. Your soul again arose to the occasion at another historic time. And, you were well rewarded for living your shameless, honestly immoral life, remember?'

Marty felt another surge of memory come flooding into her loins. She nodded, recalling one of her soul's most glorious victories over the ridiculous forces of morality. Miss Iniquity moved her dream along:

'Cleopatra was another of your soul's famous bodies. You didn't hesitate to take your rightful power. Remember the evening Caesar told you he was awaiting your husband's council to approve his submission request for grain? You were performing fellatio. You held Caesar's balls in your hands while you sucked and kissed his cock. That's when your genius thought came:

"Caesar, the world's most powerful man must not submit requests. He must demand what he wants," you spoke to the Roman.

"It's a mere formality," Caesar replied.

"It's more than a formality. It is an insult to mighty Caesar! We both know my marriage is incestuous, like my fathers' marriages were before my own. My husband-brother is an idiot dullard. I alone, of all the Ptolemies, have the mind and strength of will to rule. My soul was created to be immoral and given to whoring; and to rule, by my rightful ancestral Alexander The Great's blood lineage. I make no apologies for my immoral self. I desire all the world's wealth and power for my own. It is mine, by my right of birth from Alexander, ruler of all the world; and I have no shame or inhibition in seeking it. The only reason my brother-husband rules, instead of me, is that he was born with a penis, and I was not. If I ruled Egypt, your mere wish would be my demand. The Pharaoh's council would be abolished."

"What do you propose, Cleopatra?" Caesar kissed your lips while his hand plied your vagina, remember?' Marty nodded. She remembered.

"Do you enjoy kissing my breasts, Caesar? Do not my sex tastings make me more desirable for you than dull Calpurnia, your Roman wife? Do not my orgasms bring life and lusts into the loins *of my mighty Caesar? Would Caesar not wish to have me in his bed, always? And, more, be rid of your nuisance wife, Calpurnia? Is my love not worth far more than hers? You know my body would always please you more than hers. Could the crown of Egypt ever be worth less than a mere cousin wife?"*

"Of course. Cleopatra, you are the most delicious morsel in all the world. You possess my thoughts and my soul. My sex and mouth are your love slaves. I await your every request. What do you wish of me?"

"Answer me. Why should you not have me; and rule the world with Egypt as your obedient vassal state? Why should the world's greatest conqueror settle for less than me and all of Egypt? Why must Caesar wait for his requests to be approved by my idiot brother and his counsel of fools? I say: It is your right to rule the entire world. You should possess me, the world's tastiest morsel, and its most notorious whore. I should live to pleasure only you. After we marry under Ptolemy laws, Caesar will rule both Egypt, and me; and the entire world. You would request no more. Caesar would demand."

"But your brother is king and ruler of Egypt, by his Ptolemy birthright."

"Don't be silly, great Caesar. We must not stand on details. If Caesar were to give me my brother's penis and his balls, he would no longer be qualified to rule. I alone would then possess the Alexander birthright and become Queen. You and I would marry; and love openly before the entire world. Egypt's power and riches, and my body and love, would be owned by Caesar."

"What would you have me do with your brother?"

"Present me with his gift of birthright. Take his penis and his balls from him and give them to me. Make me Queen of Egypt and your wife. Then let the Nile crocodiles make better use of the remains of my brother's body than he ever has."

Iniquity spoke again:

'*Remember, only two days later you received a silken sachet purse. The centurion who delivered it told you it was a gift to you, complements of mighty Caesar. It contained your brother's penis and his testicles. His body was never found. You purified Caesar, honoring him and absolving him of all guilt or wrongdoing when he ejaculated in your vagina. Your intimacy freed him from all restraints to his ambitions and you became Queen of Egypt.*

'*Later, when your younger brother came into puberty, by Ptolemy Law, he was to become Egypt's rightful king. By then, Caesar had been murdered in the Roman Senate. Like you seduced Caesar and persuaded him to murder your older brother, you also seduced Marc Anthony and purified him with your whoring. He, like Caesar before him, accepted your ways. He obeyed you and honored your requests. He murdered your younger brother and your younger sister, Arsinoe. You had all your siblings murdered to make sure you had no challengers to your throne. You cavorted with Marc Anthony, as you had with Caesar. You pushed both of their Roman wives far from their minds, fornicating openly, shamelessly; purifying both men from any sense of guilt; taking your rightful place as their favorite, most loved whore; displacing their wives. Your shameless, murderous whoring accomplished your hold on power over the entire world, remember?*"

Marty nodded. Ancient memories lifted from the fog of her soul's memories. Miss Iniquity again spoke in Marty's dream:

'*Carl's wife also deserved her fate. She dared to oppose you. Like other souls before hers, your soul dispatched hers. Feel proud and accomplished in the rightness of your murder and your purification of her husband. Your soul used hypnosis for the first time. You were innovative, daring, cunning, competent, and ruthless. And, always, you acted in keeping with your obsession for results. Congratulations!*

'*Never forget when your soul was also the soul of Queen Isabella's, of Spain. You perfected your murder craft of poisoning to dispatch your older brother and become heir to the throne of Castile; and you craftily arranged alliances and poisonings. You purified Ferdinand and bonded his talents to your righteous cause, so that you and Ferdinand could forge a unified Spain. Remember?*

"Ferdinand, we will rule all Iberia, Castile, Leon, Aragon, and Segovia, after you drive out the Moors." Marty's soul heard Isabella commanding Ferdinand.

"Your brother, then my father. You are a most crafty murderess, my love. Would you poison me as well?" Ferdinand equivocated. His was the weaker soul.

"No need, my love. You have a greater duty to me than being useless in death. I need your pure semen to seed me with children for the thrones of Europe. I need you to drive out the Moors from Spain; then, to drive the Turks from Italy; then, the world will be ours."

"And while I do these duties?"

"I must be true to my honest soul, my love. I am an unrepentant whore and I must whore as I please. I must spread my exemplary intimacy far, to insure the purity and loyalty of my courtiers and the Vatican's Borgia, Pious the Sixth, to my crown. Accept that my promiscuity facilitates our power; and the future status of your progeny. They shall become kings and rulers of Europe. Be pleased and grateful that you have married the world's greatest, most glorious; and history's most immoral whore. And, always remember to uphold my faux image as Spain's virtuous, righteous Queen. Remove the tongue of anyone who dares to mock me, insult me, or dispute my claims of virtue. Murder all dissidents. Decapitate them. Put their heads on spikes."

"I am yours, my greatest, beautiful, adoring love; my queen. I am in your eternal service; and, I shall do as you command me. No one who disputes your virtue shall live." Ferdinand acquiesced to serve his wife and queen.

Miss Iniquity continued:

'You then freely whored with Ferdinand and your devoted lover companion consorts; while pretending for your subjects to be monogamous and pious, as recorded by your court historians. You gleefully cavorted in your castles while you listened with pleasured ears to the murdered cries of thousands of conversos, Jews, and Muslims whom you ordered burned alive at the stake. You launched genocides and rewarded your executioners with titles, lands, and sexual favors. You feigned piety while you received word of the thousands of death sentences and brutal executions at the auto da fe, taking place outside your castles' walls. You reveled in the reports of the tortureds' agonies, suffered by those who opposed your rule, or your faith. Then, you returned to your pleasures of cunnilingus, given you by your eager consorts; and to the fellatios you eagerly performed on them.

'When you and your court met Columbus in Barcelona, after he returned from the New World, you received him in good faith. He brought you gifts of gold, precious stones, exotic new world plants and handsome Native American men, dressed in their finery. You were joyous. You treated him as an equal; and you freely consorted with him and the Native men for weeks. You purified them and cemented their loyalties to you. You celebrated life. You proclaimed that new life and its new beginnings come from cock, vagina, and conquest. And, you honored your proclamation by reveling in orgy after orgy; night after night. Visions of untold riches and power made you joyous. Your revelry was unbridled. Perhaps that was the only mistake your whoring soul ever made, for you contracted syphilis-based ague from those days of carefree, uninhibited revelry.

'In good faith you commissioned Columbus a second, much larger expedition with instructions to the flotilla to treat the Native Americans kindly and with loving intimacy. You could not know until months and years later that these loving, intimate liaisons you championed would unleash syphilis on Europeans when those *expeditions returned; or that your intimacy seekers would unleash smallpox on the Native Americans. Once you discovered the nature of your own disease state and deduced the cause of it, you blamed your condition on Columbus; and you made certain that his discoveries would become marginalized and his life trivialized. You displayed a vengeance and a determination to never be bested, by anyone, for any reason, even for their honest mistakes.*

'You carried on your affairs of State as best you could during your eleven declining years. From the rivers of gold that flowed to you from the New World, you easily afforded the penalty fees of indulgences and dispensation payments you made to keep your Vatican Pope securely locked in your pocketbook. History and your faith wrote kindly of you. Your transgressions against morality are well secreted. While you performed your fellatios and orgies, your soldiers joyfully put their swords to millions of infidels, driving them from your peninsular kingdom and making it a safe bastion for your whoring copulations. They brought you plundered gold and treasure while you pretended to be pious, plotting your path to power over your country and your faith.

'And, you outdid all whores who ever went before you when you unleashed your conquistadores to murder millions of innocent Native Americans. Your warriors were spurred on to glory by visions of your magnificent whore lust and your immense appetite for wealth and power. You let no peoples or religions, nor blood on your hands, nor pious religious constructs stand in your way to becoming the most powerful and wealthiest person in the world, remember?'

Marty nodded; a wan smile crossed her lips. Miss Iniquity's exhortations prompted a deep-seated recall from the sixth premonition sense that resided in Marty's deepest core of being. She had a sudden epiphany. She remembered the adrenal rushes of Isabella when news of vanquished enemies arrived. It was good to be ruthless. It was joyous to conquer. It was glorious to be the world's most exalted whore. She understood Iniquity's beseeching's. She should settle for nothing less than the lineage that her soul required. She had within her the power and her will to murder by hypnosis, poison, sword, musket ball, decapitation, and burning by fire at the stake. Also, through her proxy men in arms, she was adept at torture and ruthlessness. Iniquity was pointing her way forward. She nodded in remembrance; understanding what she needed to do. To become the world's number one porn star, and receive the power, fame, and wealth which only that position would afford her, she could not allow anything or anyone to stand in her way.

'So, I am to become a notorious whore. That is my calling,' affirmed Marty, nodding her sleeping head; nodding acceptance of her destiny.

Miss Iniquity softened her voice:

'Yes, my darling; you must become that, and so much more! You are your soul's destiny child. You are perfect for your calling to become the very standard of world immorality. You will lie and withhold truths; cheat on those who love you; steal wealth and loves from others; murder those whose murders advance your glorious cause; and most certainly you will covet and act upon your impulses to covet. You will have no guilt about the things you do or the lives you affect. Pay no claptrap homage rites to any god. You are destined to be your own god. Followers hunger to worship a god. I have reposed their hunger within your immoral soul. Feed your immorality to them. They will worship you.

'Your soul has always been a change agent that advances humanity. Unchain your soul once again and be a change agent now. Create more porn films of orgies with black partners. In your media interviews, speak of the injustices that America's blacks have suffered. Proclaim that you are the living embodiment of the thirteenth, fourteen, and fifteenth Constitutional Amendments. Be the voice that strikes the final blow against injustice. Tell the world that *freedom from slavery, due process, and non-discrimination were still only half-measures. Tell your legion of fans that your revered vagina is the new and the true North Star; the ultimate arbiter; the new moral standard that eradicates racism and shows the world the way forward.'*

Marty was confused. She asked Miss Iniquity to explain what, specifically, she was directing Marty to do:

'Tell them what, Iniquity?'

'You must tell them that the white suburban woman has been the main beneficiary of discrimination against blacks. The white woman has the better neighborhood and schools that come with her status as a white. Proclaim that discrimination can not finally end until the white suburban housewife opens her vagina to the black man and welcomes him to procreate with her. Until white women proudly create black children into their families of white children, there will not be true racial equality. Until the ideal family has children of both races in it; going to school together; sitting in the family church pew together, there can not be genuine equality. You must encourage black men to seek liaisons with white women, in order to impregnate them. And you must, by your own example in your porn films, encourage white women to freely have intercourse with black men. And you must use your status as the world's most famous porn star to advocate that black men who rape white women be forgiven, or be given the most lenient sentences possible, for they are merely trying to redress centuries of black oppression by American whites. Does not your conscience feel that this is the morally right message?'

'Oh, Miss Iniquity, I do! And I'm certain it will be applauded by my fans. I will do it! I will use my fame to encourage white women to spread their legs and open their vaginas to black men's cocks! I will encourage every white woman to take a black lover! It's a wonderful cause; and a great reason to create more films with Marshawn and his friends. Yum!'

Mary felt a glowing warmth inside her breast. She knew she could always count on Miss Iniquity to advance her notoriety. A social mandate to create more porn films with black partners thrilled her. Yes, she told herself, she would gladly fornicate more for a worthy cause!

Miss Promiscuity chimed in:

'I just had the most delicious thought. Let's perform an orgy during the Superbowl halftime show! Marty could have group sex with seven black partners on the world's biggest stage.'

Miss Shameless concurred:

'I love that idea. The show would be broadcast live all over the world. Our fame would become legendary!'

Miss Iniquity cautioned the other voices:

'It might be too shocking to peoples' sensibilities. There will be underaged children there. There's the logistics; the legal approvals. It wouldn't be like making a porn film.'

Miss Promiscuity countered:

'Too shocking? I don't think so. Americans love their savagery and their wars. Football is merely a Colosseum-like microcosm abstraction of the mayhem that America inflicts on the world. Everyone watching the game is already intoxicated by the glorification of America's pagan blood lust.

'Baseball was once America's national sport. Those peaceful, pastoral days are gone. Football, the new national sport, heralds the population's reversion to humanity's natural, base paganism. The halftime shows already emphasize the beauty of the human body, its machinations; and frequent crotch touchings. That light paganism format does not present a far leap to reach live pornography. Black males on a single white female orgy theme would evoke a racial equality meme. It would be well received; praised as Avant Guard. Our reviews would be sensational.'

Miss Shameless joined Miss Promiscuity's argument:

'I agree. Violence, whether in foreign wars or in America's home-land, is growing. It's a bloodlust thing. Americans can't get enough of it. The population has become calloused, indifferent to human life and human suffering. Americans snicker and laugh at the mis-fortunes of others. They feel smug, seeing others being killed and maimed; all the while feeling above it all as spectators, like those who watch football. Violence against the other tribe, the other nation state, the more vulnerable human; without feeling compassion for the others' pain, is a hallmark of paganism.

'Pornography, like violence, is growing. It has, in fact, become mainstream. Like violence, Americans cannot get enough pornog-raphy. Porn stars receive our adulation. Their performances are praised. Their opinions and utterances are considered wisdom in many circles. Why? Because their fingers are on the pulse of Ameri-ca's soul as well as on its cocks. We are returning to pagan worship. And pornography is leading our way forward. Pagan worship and pagan violence go hand in hand, telling us to leave our old values behind and move boldly forward into the world of the New Moral-ity Standard. So, I, Shameless, opine that there is no obstacle to a Superbowl orgy fest that we cannot overcome. Marty's lawyers can take care of the censorship issues and the legalities of the contracts we will need.'

Miss Iniquity still had a reservation:

'But what about the children?'

Miss Shameless anticipated her:

'Those attending the game can be given eye masks, and their parents told to put the eye masks on their children during the half-time show. If the young lad doesn't wear his eye mask, it's the par-ents' fault, not ours. Parents of children and children watching on television will receive a message that instructs children to not watch. Our responsibility will be easily discharged. Besides, in our emerg-ing pagan culture, children, like pagan children of yore, should be *exposed to violence and prostitution worship from the beginning of their infancy. There must be no shame in our new social norms. Children must be raised to embrace the new morality and be full participants in it.'*

Marty's three voices then clasped hands together and agreed on their latest scheme. They would be united in their advice to Marty. She would be a committed whore to her core being; and they would proceed on their course with one unified purpose; that being to promote Marty as the world's premier; most notorious porn star.

Miss Iniquity refocused Marty's perspective; keeping her aware of who she was and her true nature as an iniquitous whore:

'Your reincarnated soul is the one you have always had. Cherish it. Be true to it. Use it to rule the world. Have no trepidations or regrets about using people or murdering them. Know that I am with you always, to guide you and strengthen your resolve. Have no fear. Live for the pleasures and wealth that life gives you. Take for the taking.

And Miss Iniquity cautioned Marty that even she did not know everything about everybody:

'But there is one man in your life whom I am uncertain about. I may be unable to help you with David. He perplexes me. All my thoughts about him are blurred and dissembled. I can't tell you whether to trust him. I simply do not know his soul. But I sense that he harbors something ominous, deeply inside himself. And that intractable something may be destined to viciously clash with your inner brightness. It may secretly resent your cavalier attitude about morality and sexual freedoms. He may be a friend and confidant to you by day; but a danger to you by night. Be cautious around David. Be alert and mindful of all he says and does. Fornicate with him, have your intimacy with him if you must, but always remember that his secret pleasures are murder and the macabre. He's a

puzzling enigmatic mystery, even to me. He is elusive and unpredictable; unlike the other men you know and control. I know you feel attracted to him; and you feel a strong compulsion to become his lover, but understand that those feelings may be dangerous to you.'

The voice of Miss Iniquity dissembled and faded into obscurity, then Miss Iniquity disappeared behind the closing hidden door that resided within Marty's mind. Miss Promiscuity, Marty's persistent, ever present, most familiar voice soon opened that same door and reappeared:

'Use your gut instincts with Fred,' affirmed Promiscuity, who had a way of pushing doubt and trepidation out of the way. She had her upbeat way of erasing Miss Iniquity's concerns and focusing Marty on the present:

'I promise you; Fred will be easy. Be bold and totally shameless when you seduce him. Don't try to disguise who you are or what you do. Just let your feelings guide you. Don't over-think such an easy conquest. The man is crazy out of his mind to hold you in his arms and love you. Everything will go smoothly for you. He'll be true to his type. He'll give you everything you ask, of that I'm certain. You'll see how easily and naturally everything happens and how confident you'll feel while seducing him this second time.'

Despite her recent conquest of Fred, and her initial routing of Petunia, Fred's wife, Marty's mind could not relax. Her emptiness feelings predictably returned after every seduction. The haunting uncertainties caused by her childhood abandonment never left her. It was rooted in her intractable trauma that she might never be worthy of genuine love. Try as she might to uproot this fear, she could never rip out its *entire* root. It would reappear and reassert itself whenever she saw people being loved or nurtured in the most common, simplest ways.

A simple hug, or a kiss or pat on the back; a certain warm smile. Any of those ordinary things could trigger Marty's insecurities and dissemble her thoughts; make her emotions flare. Sex was like her personal weed. It sprang, predictably, from her insecure root. She needed sex. She knew she needed sex. Sex magically quelled her anxieties for a time, but only for a short while. Her new seductions failed to destroy her resurgent sex-thirsty weed's root. Instead, her conquests nourished it. That was the addictive nature of her condition. The weed could never satisfy its own root. It never knew peace; never stopped growing; always needed more assurances and reassurances. It survived Marty's every seduction conquest and grew anew, reaching deeper into her soul and psyche, creating fresh cravings and a newer, larger, emptier void. The void continuously spread, like a grove of Aspen, fresh aspiring trees from the unbounded underground root. Marty's compulsion was to fill this recurring, expanding void in the only way she knew how. She needed more: more seductions, more men, more conquests, and more, much, much more sex. Her quest for sex was the Aspen grove's need to propagate; to gather more sunlight to nourish its hungry root. The flames of Marty's nymphomania raged within her inner psyche, always primed to flare up and consume everyone who revealed the slightest encouragement.

Compulsion and nymphomania had become Marty's vocal soul mates. They took on the personas of Miss promiscuity, Miss Shameless, and Miss Iniquity. They communed regularly with Marty's psyche. Her vagina was the high altar for her psychological companion voices. Sex was their communion's bread of life. They craved sex to sustain themselves while they pursued their endlessly futile quest for true love. Who next might they seduce to fill Marty's bottomless void? Where next might they reaffirm that she was beautiful, desirable to be romanced and copulated; and where might they turn next to obtain their requisite lust offerings?

Marty's thoughts reviewed her appointment schedule. They drifted away from Carl. As she slipped off to slumber, Marty's dreams turned a page. She was asleep now, smiling contentedly, knowing she would soon be with Fred. He needed to be led to chase her. That was perfect. Now that she understood his need, she could mold everything about their relationship to ideally suit herself. Love making with Fred was sweet. He was honestly open and beautiful. He was like a big kid who never grew up. She believed him when he confessed that he loved her. And he always strived to please her.

LOVER FRED

Marty had booked the coming weekend for fun time with Fred. He was a rich heir who lived in the suburbs. His wife left for Florida often, to visit her ailing mother. He was lonely. His wife, Petunia, rarely performed wifely duties. These circumstances presented Marty with a perfect situation. She'd first called Fred to introduce herself when she learned his broker had retired. They had agreed to discuss the management of his account on a weekday afternoon, while Fred's wife was away playing bridge. They had quick sex that afternoon in the master bedroom. That brief sampling of Marty's whoring whetted Fred's desire. She secured Fred's accounts and transferred his assets to David's firm. When she saw Fred's financial statements that proved his liquid worth was over seven hundred million dollars, Marty returned a second time while Petunia was away. They made love for a solid three hours. When Fred told Marty that he could never get enough of her, she asked him to please place another two million under the Firm's management, to compensate her for her time. He readily agreed. Marty made a fast thirty-thousand-dollar commission.

Marty applied her specialized proprietary methods to learn a client's financial picture. She sought to learn not just *what* her prospect was worth but also *how* her prospect achieved that worth;

and, *how* her prospect perceived his self-image. She observed things in far greater detail than lesser salesmen did; *and* she remembered them. For example, she took note that the grounds of Fred's country villa were immaculately maintained. Not one shrub was untrimmed, nor did a single dead branch burden any tree. All walkways and edgings around the palatial flower gardens were neatly trimmed. Not one errant twig or leaf sullied any surface. She surmised that Fred employed a gardener and held him to exacting standards.

New, expensive patio furniture, not yet sun-bleached, confirmed that Fred kept up appearances. When he showed her around the villa she marveled at the big game heads on his great room walls, the exotic tiger and lion skin rugs, and his wet bar with only the finest spirits displayed above it. The five sheep heads of different species on his great room wall seemed to command some special significance.

Her intuition told her that Fred's sheep head display projected his ego. She researched what she saw. Pictures told her that Fred had the world's most prized trophy sheep, there on his wall, including the most elusive, wildest, most exotic sheep in the world: the Dahl, Stone, Desert Bighorn, Rocky Mountain Bighorn, and the most difficult sheep in the world to hunt, the prized Afghan Mouflon. Fred's display messaged to his hunter friends that he was superior to them. He was that one hunter among a hundred thousand who had the determination to achieve the ultimate, hunting's Grand Slam. Fred's appetite for the finest trophies and the best liquor clued Marty that his ego would never allow him to settle for second best. He was a "hands on" type, a relentless alpha male type who sought to conquer challenges.

Those were her clues. Every man had a weakness. Heirs, like Fred for example, often felt overshadowed by their benefactors. This often gave rise to an inner compulsive need to prove their worthiness. Marty correctly assessed that Fred's compulsive need to prove himself was the underlying reason why he hunted.

Marty studied men. She made it her business to know them. She understood that all men are beholden to their cocks; and they are secretly obsessed with keeping those alter egos satisfied. But, beyond every male's obsession with his dick, Marty understood that every man had a particular hot button. Every man's behavior was responsive to his hot button driver. She noted that men waged constant battles for dominance over other men. But each man battled in his chosen venue. That's where his hot button was. Understanding that hot button was the key to understanding the man. Dueling challengers of old offered their antagonists their choice of weapons; but dueling itself was their real choice; their true hot button. Marty understood that, while modern men had evolved from dueling, the primal urge to dominate had not evolved, and it would not. It couldn't. It was naturally inbred into the male DNA. She understood, as a woman, that she needed to use that male urge to benefit herself.

Marty had a keen awareness of this primal male drive to compete. Modern men competed in civilized ways: sports, car racing, mathematics, physics, their collections, their organized warfare between nations, and so on. Rams butted heads for mating rights; but human males impressed their women and intimidated other males in these other, newer ways. But male competition was all the same to Marty. She would first learn a male's particular hot button. Then, she would methodically work to position herself as the prized object of his competitive ardor.

If her male target of interest raced cars, she would read about racing. She studied the other cars and drivers, and made suggestions about how her man could beat them. If he was a salesman, she suggested where or how to get more sales. She didn't need to be right, but she needed to show her man that she was engaged;

trying to help him. When her man succeeded, her praises boosted his ego. That created his psychological dependency on her.

ENIGMA DAVID

Marty often played lover and mother substitute to her male partners, conveniently delivering both personas in an irresistible, oversexed package. She had many ways of playing men. She could be coy, or dominating, or tempting; but none of her methods worked with David. He was the only man she could not figure out. He was different somehow. He gave no clues about needing anyone. She asked herself: Against what or whom was David competing? Was there something he needed? something he wanted to share with someone? She knew it was there. It was like a silent fury that raged inside him, but he kept it there, inside himself. He never let it out. Whatever it was, he was careful to keep a lid on it. Nothing answered her question: *What is your 'it,' David?*

What was David's *'it'*? What did he need? What did he want to do more than anything else? She sensed that he had to have an *'it'* out there somewhere, waiting to be discovered, but David deliberately kept his 'it' well hidden. He was so solitary he bordered on creepy. She often wondered about David's 'it' She guessed *'it'* was likely something dark, possibly heinous, possibly depraved. She could not put her finger on *'it,'* whatever the elusive *'it'* was. She sensed *'it'* possibly had something to do with their murders; yet, it was something even more secretive than the murders. David relished committing those, almost as much as she did. But as intimate as committing murder with him was, David never let those heinous acts bond him to her. He always held something back. That something was the 'it.' She knew that had to be true, but what was it?

Yet, a curious form of intimacy was implied between them. It was not sexual, at least not yet; but something that seemed even closer. On some level, she felt attached to David and very loving towards him. Like her, David also nurtured a character void. She sensed it. She didn't understand her own void, much less his; but she sensed David wanted her to help him fill the *'it'* of his empty darkness; or somehow help him lift a terribly painful burden, whatever *'it'* was.

She intuited that he brooded over that *'it.'* She tried to observe David whenever she had the chance, hoping he'd reveal something in a relaxed moment, like immediately after their murders. But even after he congratulated her and raved about how erotic and glorious her execution performances were, he never joined her festive celebrations afterwards. Instead, he acted like a common janitor removing the bodies and cleaning up. But why? The key to filling David's void was out there, in a murky somewhere. It secretly wanted her to find it. She felt certain about that. Several times she had coyly suggested that she and David have sex, hoping that he'd reveal his secret need, during or after.

But nothing ever happened. He never followed up on her hints. When she tried to understand a man's mind, she often closed her eyes and meditated. When she thought of most of her lovers, like Carl, or Bob, or many of her salesmen followers, she visualized bright blue skies, a running stream with pools to swim in, happy birds flitting amongst the tree branches; and a love scene, kissing her lover; and touching each other's genitals, in loving, passionate arousing foreplay.

But when she meditated about David, her mind's thoughts always conjured up something different. She visualized a dark muddy gloom pond, filled with protruding branches from dead trees. Little bubbles of oil seeped to its surface and spread-out colors of red and blue hues until they were absorbed back into the mud gloom. She waited for the pool to drain or for freshness to flow into it, but that never happened. Then, she gave up trying to understand David, until the next time.

Did he possess an endless, quiet determination to keep his clues hidden? She could only wonder. Her thoughts always came to this same impassable place. She resolved to tempt him again, when the opportune moment presented itself. Meanwhile, she slowly closed the door on her David thoughts, and opened the welcoming door to happier thoughts of blue skies, a lively stream with its beautiful pools, the fluttering birds, and her next seduction.

Fred's persona was the total opposite of David's. Fred was a much easier read. David was subtle, deceptive, shadowy, sneaky, and extremely dangerous in both business and life. Fred was open, bold, and confrontational toward other men, but also a very dangerous man in his own rite. Fred excelled in stealth and ambush kills. But she already understood him well enough. She had already successfully bedded him. After wracking her brains trying to understand David, Fred was welcome relief.

Fred was understandable. He proudly wore his hot button on his emotional sleeve. Everyone recognized it. Fred proclaimed it. He was the alpha male, the top trophy hunter of the hunt club. The tougher the challenge, the more Fred wanted it. He prided himself in conquering every challenge, solo. His clues told Marty that she shouldn't offer herself to Fred like she often did to David. Instead, she should position herself as Fred's most elusive trophy. She would let him taste her scent; then let him chase her until she captured him.

David was taking years of painstaking observation. Comparatively speaking, Fred was low hanging fruit. Marty considered her approach. She would challenge Fred; make him work hard to conquer her. She couldn't help him too much or make anything too easy. That would ruin the experience he craved. Being a man, Marty understood Fred would need some prompting to arouse his interest. She would be patient, encouraging, while letting his huge, clueless hands fumble to unzip her dress, unfasten her bra, unbutton her blouses, unsnap her teddies, and pull down her panties; all the while pretending she was amazed and exceptionally pleased out of her immoral whoring mind at his relentless, remarkable prowess.

'*Do not serve up your body on a platter,*' she reminded herself. The way to Fred's heart and money was through his ego. That ego wanted the world to recognize that he could manage everything himself. He needed to prove he could conquer every challenge alone. He never even took guides along on his hunts. He slept outside on the ground in the freezing cold, rain and snow. He had pushed himself to near exhaustion death until he got his elusive Mouflon; and then he had packed it off those twenty-thousand-foot-high mountain cliffs, by himself. He was relentless and unstoppable. This was a man who needed to take her panties off, without any help from her; otherwise, he'd lose interest.

Marty was expert at psychologically assessing the key needs of every one of her seductions. She knew her success depended upon identifying each man's hot button; his particular 'it.' She had correctly assessed her odds of success with Fred on her first visit. That seduction went beautifully. She appealed to Fred's quest for exclusivity as a vivacious, classy, coiffed, and well-dressed femme fatale. He immediately sized up Marty as another potential trophy, albeit a living one. He would chase her until she gave up. He believed he could bag her.

Marty understood Fred's needs even better than Fred did. She first let him catch her and bed her for a brief fifteen-minute tumble. She then pretended that he caught her off guard and ambushed her. That gave him a hint of what was possible; but then she pulled away and became elusive, making their future meetings conditional, leaving him wanting more of her than their first quick encounter. She cleverly put him onto her scent. He thought she was elusive prey. She intended to lead him on, until she captured him. Their chase was on.

CAPTURED

When Marty had arrived that fateful second time, she wore a tight-fitting low-cut designer cocktail dress with tiny gold studs joined by toggle loops that tenuously secured its transparent chiffon material. It only partially covered her breasts. She was dressed to kill; not Fred's ardor for her, but his thoughts of Petunia. Marty calculated that seduction was a zero-sum game. She knew only one woman could possess and control Fred. She intended to be that woman. The other woman in his life, his wife, would have to go. She proudly held her shoulders back, uplifting her breasts. Her cherry-colored nipples protruded invitingly through the flimsy material, signaled that her mouth-watering temptation buds were eager to escape their confinement behind the pesky, tissue-like gauze. Her provocative posture and inviting smile signaled that her breasts were anxious to be touched, stimulated, and toyed with by Fred's fingers; and kissed by his lips.

She wore five-inch, cherry-colored spiked heels this day. They perfectly matched the color of her buds. She believed in the suggestive power of color associations. Her hair was freshly coifed with sprinkles of gold dust that complimented the gold bracelets adorning both her arms. Her gold announced that Marty was about wealth. She loved it and craved more of it. A ten-caret ruby hung deliciously down her breasts, lodging itself securely within her luscious cleavage, signaling that she was pricey. And worth it. Her lipstick, blush, eye shadow, mascara and scents were all perfect, declaring that she was an exceptionally magnificent, exquisite femme. She came to Fred this day as eye candy, the ultimate trophy female for the ultimate alpha male who was driven to possess the greatest, most coveted, of all prizes.

Fred instantly recognized that Marty dazzled more than all his other trophies, combined. She was a far more exotic, harder to get ornament than Petunia had ever pretended to be. Marty's assumptions were exactly right. Fred's mouth watered the moment he saw her. His eyes drank in every inch of her before fixating momentarily on her garment's toggles. Marty watched his mind contemplating. He was unfastening them one by one with his hands and setting her breasts free. She was the one priceless trophy Fred did not have. And the one he knew he absolutely had to have. His eyes burned with passion's fires when they lifted to meet Marty's alluring smile. She noticed. It was time to set the terms of the chase.

"I was so relieved to hear from you, Fred," she purred. *"I was afraid something happened to you. You hadn't called me for ten whole days. Every time my phone rang, I prayed it would be you. I imagined your wife had you trapped in this big mansion all by yourself while she ran off to play bridge with her friends. I prayed that she'd go back to Florida and stay away for a whole month, playing Mahjong with her mommy. I hoped I could come and be with you. I missed you terribly, Fred. My body was crying from being without you. I needed you so badly. I wanted you to hold me, and kiss me and touch me everywhere, in all the ways that only you know how to touch me."*

"Oh, Marty, Marty, I didn't mean to deny you. I think the world of you," declared Fred. *"I didn't want to be away from you either. I called you many times but you didn't pick up. I didn't want to leave a message. It's just that my wife is home sometimes, and I didn't want her to discover our love. I don't want her to make a scene that might embarrass you. I'm falling in love with you. I told you that before.*

Please believe me. I need you. May I pour you a drink?" he made his awkward offer, unsure of what to do next.

'*Skip the preliminaries,*' whispered Miss Shameless to Marty:

'*You saw it was him calling. You only wanted to make him call back all those times to give him the feel of the chase. Now he's finally caught up with you. This is your moment. Take charge. Catch this little boy who pretends to be a big man. Make him believe he's irresistible, and that your attraction to him is genuine. Touch his face and kiss his cheek. Tell him how good he looks by the way he parts his hair, but do not muss his hair. He's a perfectionist, remember? See how perfectly his hair is parted, straight from back to front? No single hair crosses that borderline. Like every blade of his lawn grass, every strand of his hair is in its perfect place. That perfectly placed blonde hair and those piercing blue eyes give him that Bald Eagle, top predator look that he tries to cultivate. Remember to play to his ego's image.*

'*Get busy. Eagles strike swiftly and fiercely. You need him to take you quickly. Beam your "I badly need to fuck you" smile. Smile from deep inside yourself and smile that smile with your eyes as well as your mouth; and let the tip of your tongue show when you beam your mouth smile. He needs to imagine you want his cock in your mouth. Make him feel he needs to do his flying eagle kill dive and attack you, like you're helplessly vulnerable bait meat, being offered on a string. Be your ravenous, appetizing best. Enjoy it while he takes you and devours you. And when you've finished making love with him be sure you tell him that it was absolutely beautiful, perfect; the most wonderful, most perfectly complete, and thoroughly enjoyable love making that you've ever experienced. He's a perfectionist, remember.'*

"*I'm not much for drinks, Fred,*" responded Marty, licking her lips with her most enthusiastic, winsome smile. "*I'd much rather be taken to your bedroom. It's been so long since we played. I want to celebrate just being with you again. I'd love you to make me feel like I'm your conquered woman. I need to have that feeling that you've captured me and that now you own me. I want you to order me to suck your cock, Fred. There, I'm embarrassing myself at my own lack of modesty, but I've said it. My urge to suck you is overwhelming me. I need you to order me to please you. Tell me that I need to prove that I can be worthy of you. Attack me. Conquer me, Fred. Squeeze my soft ass with your huge hands while you fuck me. Please ravage me mercilessly and dominate me. Show me that you're the only man in the world who impose his manly ways on me.*

"*I'm being honest, Fred. That's what I want more than anything. I need to know you're a dominant man's man. I need to taste your beautiful, glorious cock in my mouth. I need to feel it getting hard. I want you to be naughty with me. Pinch me and slap my tush hard. I want to feel like you own me. I'm dying to suck you, Fred. I haven't been able to think of anything else since I saw you. Make me feel what it's like for a real man to have his way with me, Fred,*" she whispered with her kitten purr voice, while her hand softly rubbed the front of his trousers.

As they entered the bedroom Marty picked up the framed picture of Fred standing with his arm around Petunia.

"*Fred, darling, may I please put this in a drawer? She looks so plain and tawdry standing beside you. I don't like seeing anything that detracts from your manly image.*" Watching Fred smile and comply without any hint of objection, Marty knew she was well on her way to displacing his wife.

'*Petunia must be an idiot,*' Marty thought to herself. '*She leaves Fred for weeks at a time while she plays board games with her mommy. I can't believe she leaves him alone like this. How stupid! It's almost too good to be true. But it is true. It's the perfect set up. Thank you, Miss Promiscuity, Miss Shameless, and Miss Iniquity. Please help me stay alert and focused on his money.*'

Fred visualized his friends' jealousies when they would see Marty on his arm. He grinned. Their imaginations would run wild, wondering what his new life with a notorious porn star was like. Now in bed, Fred's back and head were propped up high on pillows. He was in a perfect position to watch Marty while she sucked and conversed with his cock. Marty loved what she was doing. She held a deep and abiding affection for male penises. While performing her heavenly fellatio she lavished praises upon Fred's object of her attentions. She earnestly took his cock into her confidence, as if she were conversing with a real person. She complemented it:

"You are such a tasty, handsome, and proud penis. You are a beautiful king. You stand very proud and very tall above a world of inferior pawns," she spoke lovingly to his member. *"You're a strong champion; a prize winning, proud cock, aren't you? May I call you Mr. King? Would you like to be my Mr. King? Would Mr. King like to help a playful, naughty girl have some fun? Does my tongue feel good to you, my king? Do you like how you feel while my lips kiss your head? You have a very beautiful head, Mr. King. Do you like how my tongue tickles your circumcision ring? Does that excite you and make you even harder? I hope that makes you happy, dear King. Do you like how you feel while my lips are sucking you and my fingers are stroking you? Do you like how I'm doing that now? Is my mouth pleasing you, my wonderful king? I hope you love it while I lick your balls, my wonderful king. I adore your balls, dear king.*

"Oh, now you've gotten very big and very hard. That's very good. I'm so proud of you, my king. You're such a big, handsome penis. I've falling in love with you. We could do so many fun things together. I hope Fred will let us play together often. You do know that you're very big and very special, don't you? I've often dreamed of having you inside me, exploring me and thrusting into me. Could we please have some fun, today? I want to feel your bigness everywhere inside

me. I want your bigness to touch all of my nerve endings and make me gush inside. Won't you please enter me and play inside of me for a while? I'd love feeling your hot creamy cum filling up the whole inside of me. Would you like to do that with me? Would you like to come inside me and feel how slippery warm I am? I'd love for you to come inside me. That would make me feel wonderful. Won't you please come inside me? It's much warmer inside me. You'll love inside me, I promise."

Her persuasive banter with his penis entertained Fred in ways his wife could never have imagined. Like an eagle, he attacked. He turned her over and pushed her down on the bed, like she was vulnerable prey. Quickly, he spread her thighs. Mr. King's head rubbed his intentions against Marty's outer vaginal lips and noticed how slippery warm and creamy she was.

"Oh, my wonderful proud king! I feel you. You are so wonderful and beautiful! I feel you demanding that I open myself to you, so you can come inside me and ravage me. You feel so dominant, so commanding, Mr. King. I'm afraid I cannot resist you. I'm afraid I feel so helpless and powerless when you want me like this. I simply cannot refuse your demand."

Marty's hand positioned Fred's penis perfectly for entry. *"Oh, my dearest King, please make me your love slave. Take me. I cannot resist your amazing power. Yes, have your way with me."*

Fred penetrated her. His hands ravaged her hair, then they grasped her baby soft, smooth, fuck-loving tush and pulled her close, all the way, tightly, up to him. He felt that moment of intimate triumph that the man inside him had to have. Marty smiled at Fred and kissed him, knowing that she was giving him hot, passionate sex, exactly what he needed. He adored Marty's shameless abandon; her unapologetic willful whoring. He loved her casual lack of modesty. He assessed her as the rarest sort of woman; one who fully understands the sexual role a woman completes in her man's life. He objectified her as a sex goddess. His personal sex goddess. She excelled in every aspect of her world of sexuality.

She was so much unlike Petunia, who dithered endlessly about trivial household matters, their social calendar, and their charitable giving. Marty was his idea of the ultimate trophy woman. She had poise, charm, looks and limitless sex appeal. She employed all of her many attributes, shamelessly; without equivocation and without a moral compass. She was a purposeful whore; a very splendid and beautiful one who excelled at her tradecraft.

And Fred, her latest conquest, had already become obsessed over her. His mind became flooded with thoughts of her; of the two of them together, doing intimate things together; uncaring about anything or anyone else but their shared pleasures. He wanted more of Marty, sexually; and for show. And, to Marty's good fortune, Fred was basically a kind hearted man. He wanted to be good to Marty and he wanted her to be happy with him.

Marty understood what was taking place inside Fred's mind. She was in her element. After playing her "play inside me" games with Fred's penis, she sensed he was ready for her special treat. She changed positions and straddled his legs. She patiently sucked his cock again, coaxing its semen eruption, followed by repeated pulses of thick, creamy white. She swallowed all of it, then smiled her most sincere loving smile.

"I loved sucking your beautiful Mr. King more than anything else in the world, Fred" she cooed softly while still holding and stroking it. *"While sucking him. I felt like I was becoming your conquered woman. I loved how that made me feel like your love slave. I felt like you owned me. I experienced the most wonderful love making I've known in my entire life, Fred,"* she lied. *"It was so beautiful and memorable. I know I will never forget it. I loved every minute of it! I especially loved sucking Mr. King after he became intimate with*

me. I loved how he gushed and gushed inside my mouth, Fred. That was unforgettably beautiful!"

Marty flashed her most endearing, sincere, *'I really love making love with you, and I can't wait to do that again; I hope we'll do this again and often,'* smile.

She told Fred they needed to make love much more often. She spoke the truth. She loved him enough to include him as one of her primary lovers, and she especially loved sucking his proud cock.

'See if he's willing to please you. It's important. It will bind him more closely to you and make him feel privileged to pleasure you.' whispered Miss Shameless.

"Fred, darling, will you help a playful girl feel her sexiest, most revealing, shameless best? Sometimes a girl just needs to feel her lover believes she's special and appreciated. Would you help me feel that way, Fred? Please?" Marty whispered with her doe eyes, pleading for a yes response.

"Yes, of course, anything you ask," was Fred's willing response.

Sensing Fred was in a playful mood, Marty pleaded in a soft, lusty voice,

"Would you be my dearest, my sweetest lover, Fred? Would you rub me with my lilac scented baby oil? Would you rub it softly into my body; everywhere, especially into all my crevasses; and onto my breasts, my nipples, my tummy, my vagina, and my legs and back; everywhere? I'd love having my entire body feeling your big strong hands touching me everywhere. I want every part of my body to know your strong powerful hands want me. I'd like to feel special, Like I'm one of your trophies. I want to feel like you are pleased you've conquered me and you are proud to have me.

"Make me feel like you own me, Fred. Control my body. Touch me, squeeze me, pinch me, and kiss me everywhere. Treat me like

you own me, like I'm a special, prized trophy; and you've finally conquered me; and now you can do to me whatever pleases you."

Fred slathered the scented oil over every inch and crevasse of Marty's anatomy. His hands and fingers lingered on her breasts and nipples; and they visited the waxed flesh mounds of her vagina. His hands discovered a novel kind of fresh confidence in their new love making role. Laying his hands upon Marty's body; touching her everywhere while she sexily stretched and purred and preened; while probing and pleasuring the sensitive realms of her tattooed vagina, lifted Fred's manly confidence.

He followed Marty's suggestions, getting his hands and psychic Zen into a wholesome unity of oneness with her body; mastering the subtleties of erotic love making. He was achieving an inner resonance, tuned to Marty's feelings of uninhibited pleasures. He paid rapt attention to every nuance that pleased the seductive vixen. Marty's response subtleties, he discovered, were more intriguing than the detailed planning chores that went into his hunts. He recorded to his memory Marty's every subtlety distinct expression; her every smile, moan, giggle, and gasp; her every softly uttered purring groans of pleasure; every stretch and wriggle of her sensuous body, and every affirming word she whispered. He studied the ways she rolled her irises into her eyelids and the slightest movements of her lips. He was becoming obsessed with capturing every essence of her sensuous love making and pleasure takings.

And he became smitten with his thoughts of possessing her. He knew she was a different sort of challenge than his trophy Mouflon. But it was the challenge itself that beckoned him. He would rise to the occasion. He would do whatever he needed to do to succeed. He willed himself to become masterful at pleasing her. He, while he slathered her body with oils, crossed the commitment threshold. He would win her!

He commanded his very soul to abandon all other interests and focus on this one great prize. He would rise to the challenges of love. He would love her with an ardor that would bind her love to him. He would learn and know every minutia about her body and her ways; and he would remember every touch that pleased her. He studied her now with even greater intensity than he had studied his elusive prized Mouflon. Fred was tracking his greatest prize.

'This is excellent,' whispered Miss Shameless to Marty:

'His hands are imprinting their memories of their touchings of you everywhere on your body. He is hand-eye coordinating and imprinting you into his psyche. He is erasing all romantic cognitions of his wife from his amygdule; and establishing your soft voice and your smiling face and pleasing body as the complete persona most associated and trusted by his hippocampus. His freshly generated neurons need reinforcement now. You're making major strides. His mind is flooding with obsessive lust for you. You will soon possess all his thoughts.

'Be bold now. Be proud of your bountiful sexuality. Be joyful that he appreciates you. Smile boldly. Cavort. Chuckle. Tease. Kiss and touch. Be delighted that he wants to share his intimacy lust with you. Be positive and encouraging. Be assuring him of the rightness of what you are doing. Tell him what he is doing with your body is good and wonderful; and that you are delighted by every touch, every kiss. Dispel all doubts and uncertainties. Be glorious and shameless and uninhibited in your immorality. Be praising of his manliness and courage. Assure him that his love making is beautiful and wholesome; and that it is his natural right to have these idyllic, sensuous times with you. You'll soon possess his entire limbic zone. Keep going. Be shameless.'

Marty positioned her oiled, naked body atop Fred's. She French kissed him lovingly while slipping his reawakened penis back inside her vagina. Then she softly twerked her tush while moving her hips from side to side. His penis felt wildly erotic sensations that it had never known before. The long, slow, sensitivity slides, the passion heat of Marty's vagina while it moved, side to side; forwards and backwards, stroking his shaft, first grinding down hard on it; and then lifting herself back up, ever so slowly; always teasing it, coaxing it to beg her to never stop.

When she sensed Fred's second ejaculation was near, she sat bolt upright and moved her pelvis tightly against his shaft, taking all of him deeply inside her. She fondled the testicles of her conqueror with one hand, while stroking her clitoris rhymically against his captive cock.

Her eyes smiled deeply into Fred's, convincing him that their adulterous coupling was perfectly natural and wholesome. Her mouth smiled with a happy robustness, communicating expressively that their new, immoral liaison was simply the beautiful, wondrous, healthy joining of their passion parched souls. Her innocent eyes assured Fred that they would never have cause to concern themselves with anything other than their pleasures.

Marty's ribald, shameless moans and belly laughs brushed away and expunged any guilt or reservations that Fred may have felt about their liaison. Marty's vagina slathered her delightfully hot slipperiness joyously over Fred's cock. Her pelvis pressured it gently against her experienced clitoris. Feelings of goodness and wholesomeness vanquished all thoughts of wrongdoing from Fred's mind. Marty's crafted expressions, kisses, hugs, touches, and sounds gave Fred all the rationale he ever needed.

He felt rightly moral and natural to make love with Marty in his wife's marital bed. This second time his spurts would come smoothly and naturally, like they were responding to the honest beckoning's of nature; and, they would be. Making love with this fantastic woman, this new love, this buxom, beautiful fun-loving whore, now became Fred's God-given right! She made him feel like he was the King of the entire world; the way he knew he should feel. It was only right that she should be his, that they should freely enjoy their moments together like they were enjoying at this moment; and often. After all, everyone knew that he was the greatest hunter in the club!

He sat upright and wrapped his arms around her, pulled her tightly against him; then he pressed his face deeply into her breasts. Such loving softness! The traces of her heavenly moisture on his lips were like morning dew on a mountain hillside; special. A miraculous wonder of nature. She was his trophy goddess now; heaven sent! She was everything he lusted for when he felt alone at home or lonely on a hunt. He clung to his newly prized, wondrous lust bundle. Nubile, firmly fleshed, lust filled; available and all for him! Fred was falling in love. Marty was no longer a whore! She was so much more than that. She was his goddess!

Oh, certainly Fred knew that Marty was wanton, immoral, and cavalier about intimacy; but Fred easily ignored those cautions. She was here! She was with *him* now! That was all that mattered, wasn't it? That suddenly made everything about Mary's immorality, moral and good by the very nature of love. Everything about her was suddenly enlightening and beautiful and glorious! And so very convincingly right! Of course, what they were doing this day was right, perfectly right. Yes, it was!

Making love so leisurely, so unconcernedly, so uninhibited like this was all about the goodness and blessings of life. Yes, it was! What was life about, anyway? What was wrong or guilt stirring about destroying his marriage to Petunia? Why, nothing at all! Why should that trouble him in the slightest? Why should he not shed her like a snake sheds its old skin? Why, no reason not to! None at all! If not with this joyous nymph, then with whom or with what? If he could not, in his own mind and new skin feel free to be with this woman he suddenly loved; then why bother with life at all?

He tenderly held Marty in his arms. She was everything Petunia wasn't. Marty was perfectly fine with what they were doing. He adored that about her. Her morals were not troubled by their adultery in the slightest. That was what was so wondrous about her. His betrayal of Petunia did not concern her in the slightest. That sinfulness about her titillated him; appealed to his reverence for predators and his disdain for prey.

She fully approved of his betrayal of Petunia; encouraged and enabled it. She championed it and rewarded him with her kisses and pleasing laughter for doing it. Her chortling laughs mocked Petunia. That sense of unsympathetic, willful conquest that Fred recognized in Marty recalled from within his memories the behaviors he observed in lion prides and hyena packs after their kills. The casual, unpretentious ways they joyfully savaged the bodies of their unfortunate weak victims, while feasting upon them, fascinated Fred. He admired predators and their behaviors, because he understood that was the way of life and survival; and it was a necessary part of living.

That understanding about life made everything right about these passions that Fred felt for Marty. In Fred's eyes, Marty could do no wrong. She was an apex predator of a different sort, that's all. She had all the right tools to make her kills. Not claws and dagger-like teeth; but softness, guile, sensuality; and a heavenly face and body. She was angelic, loving, lovely and thoroughly immoral and free of guilt or remorse; the mortal enemy of marriage and moral Christendom.

And Fred respected Marty. She was a killer, like himself; but of a different kind, who hunted a different kind of victim; who plied her skills not in the world's wildernesses, but in its boudoirs. She didn't use a rifle or a bow and arrow. She used her charm, her body, her delicious cock loving lips and her sensational, sensuous fuck-loving vagina. Fred and Marty. Their coming together this way could not be bad. Their union could not be immoral when applying the real-world standards of survival of the fittest; the standards of the animal kingdom that Fred respected and accepted. That made what was happening between him and Marty perfectly moral. It could not be otherwise; not while she loved him like this.

Marty's immorality, in the civilized world's notions of good and evil, arose from her natural innocence and her natural nympho libido. Therefore, her behaviors could not wrong; could not be anything other than moral and good. Immoral? She simply could not be. She and all she did had to be good, beautiful, and healthy. Besides, he *LOVED* her.

So, what if others opined that she had no morals? He didn't care. And why should he? He didn't need then. He didn't need them when he hunted alone and he didn't need them now. To hell with them! With every pairing of his lips to Marty's; every movement of his arms that held her body close to his; every thrust of his cock inside her hot slippery love sheath; every breath she breathed upon his chest; every touch of her fingers, brought visions of a lion pride into his mind. They were casually tearing apart a large antelope they had killed; feeding their need for life upon its hapless body. They were unconcerned with its feelings as they ripped open its gut and devoured its liver and heart. They thought it only natural that they tore its limbs asunder and ripped chunks of flesh from its body. They displayed a certain enjoyment about this process of life.

Occasionally one lion would pause to lick the face of another or rub its body against another's body. Life and survival brought happiness to the pride. Doing what came naturally to live was a good thing and they enjoyed it. Fred was in his own, man created paradise with Marty. He was doing what came naturally to him and to her; making love. He felt no concerns or remorse about what they were doing. Like the lion pride, he was thoroughly enjoying himself and had every confidence that Marty was enjoying her experience as well. He had every intention to continue making love with this lovely, promiscuous whore as long as she would have him and as long as he was able.

And Petunia? Like the lion pride had every intent of eating every morsel of their antelope, Fred had every intent, fully shared with Marty, of devouring every vestige of marriage to Petunia. Lions often will laboriously lie near their kill carcasses, unconcerned that it will somehow resurrect itself and escape from the damage they've inflicted upon it. In similar fashion, Fred and Marty would casually, unconcernedly, displace Petunia's living presence from their lives. Her feelings? Of no concern. Her social status? Reduced to a chimera of what it once was; and not Fred's concern. He lived in the world where lions lived, where life and death were real; where the strong devoured the weak.

Now, with Marty's help, his mind found itself free of all concerns about Petunia or anything else that might distract or dissuade him from his single-minded pursuit of trophy Marty. He hung on every word she spoke. He responded to her every touch. His ears resonated to the sounds of her soft, sensuous, purrs and whispered voice:

"Yessss, Fred, YESSSS, YESSSSS! Oh, that feels soooo gooood! YES! Ohhh, love me, love me, OH, YES, FUCK ME! YESSSS! Please let me have you. Please give it to me. I want it. I want you to fuck me. I love having your penis inside me. I absolutely love it!

"Will you come inside me? Will you please come inside me, Fred? I want to feel your hot creamy semen shooting inside me. I love how that feels. Please give me that feeling. I want you to fill me up. Yes, that's it. I feel you inside me. Oh, Fred, that feels so good. Stay inside me. Yes, there, that's it. Stay, Fred, please stay inside me. Right there!

Yes, that's it. Push, YES, push hard and far up inside me! Can you feel how much I want you? Do you have any idea how good you're making me feel?

"Oh, please, please make love with me. Yes, love me like that, yes, just like that. I love how you're loving me. *That feels SOOO GOOD! Can you tell how much I love your penis inside me? I do, Fred. Absolutely I do. I love it SOOO MUCH! Oh, that's SOOO BEAUTIFULLY WONDERFUL! YES, I can feel you. You're coming inside me now.*

"Oh, Fred. You are such a wonderful man, such a beautiful man. You are a wonderful, fantastic lover. I love what you're doing to me. I can feel you coming again. You're SOOO hot. Oh, Fred, this is so marvelous and beautiful. Do you have any idea how wonderful you're making me feel? Oh, yes, give it to me. Give me all of it. I love how I feel while we're making love. That's it, Fred. Push hard against me. Harder and higher up, Fred. YES! I can really feel you now. You're coming some more. I can feel you. You're coming. That's so beautiful. You are so marvelous, Fred. Oh, Fred, you're sooooo good to me. I lovvvve your penis. I just love it; totally love it. That was so beautiful. I feel SOOO good."*

She performed rapid, pulsing Kegel squeezes upon Fred's captivated shaft while kneading his testicles. After he finished, Marty retreated to the water closet, freshened herself and returned. Miss Shameless offered Marty her summary of the seduction:

'He's shown you he wants to please you by rubbing you in oils. He also pushed harder and higher when you asked him to. He pleased you more when you asked him to lift higher, and then he stroked your clit perfectly. Notice, he's given you no indication that he's ever performed cunnilingus.

'So, pace yourself with him, but be persistent. You want your pheromone tastes and smells permanently imprinted on his taste buds, his scent receptors, and flooding his limbic zone. You want to

saturate his emotional center and bond him to you, so that when-ever he suffers setbacks; or receives insults, feels rejections or per-ceived slights, he will come to you seeking emotional comfort. His ego desperately needs a safe place. Be his welcoming refuge from every trouble that arises in his world. And, as you well know, trou-bles routinely arise in every human life.'

Marty hearkened to the wisdom of Miss Shameless while con-tinuing her soulful French Kisses.

"Fred darling, would you please, please kiss my sex? Please, I'd love you to do that with me. I know it's a very bold request to make, but I feel so much love for you, Fred. I feel so good about myself, so right about our love; and I've become completely shameless and uninhibited when I'm with you. I believe our feelings for each other would reach an even higher level of intimacy if you would please do that. I want to have that completely intimate feeling with you Fred. I'm all refreshed now. I am so ready for you and wanting you. I so much want you to love kissing me that way."

"Yes, of course, Marty. Anything you'd like." Fred was willing to learn the things that pleased his newest trophy.

Marty was pleased with Fred's response. She patiently coached Fred in the art of pleasing a woman through oral sex.

"That's it, Fred. You just touched it. Can you feel it?" Fred gave an almost imperceptible nod of his head. *"That's good, Fred; really, really good. Now, Fred, I'd like you to slide your tongue over it slowly, up and down over the entire length of it. Yes, you're doing it. You're getting it, Fred. That's really good, Fred. That feels so beautiful, Fred.*

"Now, Fred, I want you to stroke the sides of it, nice and slowly; all the way up and down the entire length of it; and on both sides of it, one side after the other. Oh, Fred! You're doing that so beautifully! Can you feel how swollen I'm getting? That's how I get when I'm at the beginning of an orgasm.

"Yes! I can feel my urges getting stronger. I'm like a dam. I'm getting swollen, being filled with juices of my love for you. I'm just awaiting the moment when I release. This is going to be so wonderful, Fred. It will my first orgasm with you from oral sex. Let's fix this moment in our memories, Fred. It's such a special time for both of us.

"Now, Fred, if you can, please try stroking my clit while using the underside of your tongue. You'll need to arch your neck way back to get your face really low on me. Maybe slide a little lower on the bed to get yourself into the most comfortable position. You should fully share in the glory of my release when it happens.

"Now, Fred, lift my tush up and hold me a little elevated with your hands. That's it. Good, Fred. Now, hold my vagina tightly against your mouth while your inverted tongue slides over my clit. OHHH! YESSS! You're doing it, Fred. You are really doing it. You're doing it beautifully on your very first try.

" I love you, Fred. I totally love you. You just got it perfectly there. You are the greatest lover I've ever had, Fred. I'm so in love with you. I'm so in love with what you are doing to me. That is SOOO FANTASTIC. Oh, Fred. You have no idea how much you are thrilling me. You are sending tingles through my entire body. You're making me crazy in love with you.

"OHHH! Fred. Keep doing that. YES! Do it faster. YES! That's it, Fred. You are such a wonderful man. That's is so beautiful. My feelings are fluttering like a butterfly's wings. I'm totally loving what you're doing to me. You are bringing out such intense feelings of love in me. I love you, Fred. I love what you are doing to me. I want to purr like a happy kitten. Please, Fred, keep going. Yes, that's it. I feel myself building up to it now. Yes, I'm going to come soon. I'm almost there, Fred. Yes, Yes. YES! YES! That's it.

"OHHH! Fred, I'm coming! Fred, can you feel me? Can you taste me? That's my love for you. It's exploding, Fred. Can you feel how

I'm gushing into your mouth? This is so beautiful, Fred. Do you love how I taste? I hope you do, Fred. I'd love doing this often, I just love it so much, Fred. You're such a wonderful love, Fred. You are my truest love, ever. Oh, Fred! I do love you SOOO very much. That was SOOO beautiful. I hope you liked tasting my love. Was it as good for you as it was for me? Was it good, Fred? Was it beautiful?"

"Yes, Marty, it was wonderful. I loved doing that with you. I could feel you enjoying it. You were so right about how it would make us feel closer. I've never felt that close to anyone before. I love you now, more than ever; more than I've ever loved anyone."

Soon after Fred had located Marty's clitoris, he was mastering his loving tongue strokes, titillating her clit's sides and base with erotic adoration, acquiring his taste for her, when it suddenly rushed up on her. It shocked her that a man who had never before performed cunnilingus could possibly be so expert at oral sex. But he was! Marty was ecstatic!

Fred was a true champion. He prided himself at being the best at everything he did. Oral sex was no exception. He was the best she'd ever had. She had never expected or experienced an orgasm quite like it. When she began flowing, he continued stimulating her. He got into the deepest pleasure connections her mind had ever known. She loved it. She wanted it to continue forever. Her thoughts sublimated into fantasies.

Wild horses ran through Marty's mind. She saw their muscles rippling and felt their hot snorting breaths on her neck as they galloped across the prairie. Then she came, as if lava flowing from a volcano, belching out its fluid spurts and oozing its hot slipperiness inside her sex. Her whole world started spinning. She lost her orientation and all sense of where she was. Her mind was whisked away as if in an airplane now; racing down an imaginary runway, gathering speed, taking off; now soaring, barrel rolling in a wild upward spiral toward the sun. The intensity of her orgasm grew stronger and stronger. She held Fred's head and mouth tightly close against her vagina, never wanting him to stop.

Suddenly her airplane vanished. In its place was a torrent of foaming, gushing flows as if from a damn burst. She writhed wildly. The pleasure of her orgasm consumed her body. She entered a delirium state of passion's most intense pleasures. Then, suddenly, tigers leaped up from the grasses with their claws and mouths open trying desperately to capture her passions; never releasing them. Her perfectly manicured nails dug hard into Fred's neck and shoulders.

She knew he must not be allowed to stop, no matter how intensely she felt her pleasure; how impossible controlling her passion bursts had become. Then, her wild tigers suddenly fell away. She felt an avalanche of snow suddenly superheat; then blast explosively away from the mountainsides within her. It swelled into a great river that cascaded over a Niagara waterfall. The power of the burst caused her to writhe uncontrollably and scream like wildcats scream into the understanding night when they make their love.

Fred was hers now; unquestionably hers. She had bonded him to her pleasures; to meet her sexual needs and be devoured by her lust passions whenever they arose. Her conquest of Petunia's bed and husband was now nearly complete. She would savor this victorious orgasm often in her memory. And, she needed more; because she believed there was still more.

She thrust her sex hard against Fred's mouth, desiring that more; thrashing her head from side to side on the bed, clawing at the sheets, trying desperately to keep her body anchored to earth, but failing terribly. Another powerful, blast-burst orgasm exploded from deep inside her. Animal lust erupted again, unchecked. Now screaming while her body convulsed, her mind flew to the moon and back to earth again; reentering fast, crazily fast; but then slowly, peacefully, gently, she felt the return of her inner calmness and satisfied peace, at last.

She had just experienced the most unexpected, most wonderful, continuous orgasm experience, ever in her life. Her flow eruption had finally slowed; but she felt there was still more. She wanted to savor it, hold fast to it never let go of it, keep it fixed permanently there in her pleasured limbic zone. She held Fred's mouth against her vagina, while they both treasured their profound intimacy.

Fred was smitten. He had experienced passage through a life changing experience. His mind had opened the gateway to Marty's gardenia scented Elysium field. His soul willingly followed. It inhaled and swallowed her gardenia scented purity; tasted life's most undeniable truth; then surrendered itself to become dissolved in her eternity. He would love and cherish Marty for the rest of his life. He bonded himself to her. Finally, he was one with his ultimate trophy. He adored his new prize. Marty had transformed herself, from trophy to goddess.

Fred prided himself on his accomplishments. He approached life as if it was a perpetual, endless challenge, not to be savored and enjoyed, but to be conquered. When he was a young boy, he had joined the Boy Scouts. As a scout, he excelled at achievement, earning every merit badge which that youth development program offered. He carried his quest for achievement and conquest into his passion for hunting. To obtain each trophy head, Fred drove himself mercilessly to understand the nature and habit and habitat of every animal whose head he would mount on his walls.

Fred did not do his hunts on game farms. He did them in the wild, by himself, without a guide. When Fred looked upon one of his fifty animal heads, he could reflect feelings that shared with his conquered quarry their profound understanding. When mounting an animal's head, Fred believed he was honoring that animal's essential essence and himself. The head signified that Fred and his animal specimen had, together, achieved their ultimate understanding and unity. Each animal was great; magnificent, the best of its kind. Each head represented painstaking study, planning, arduous work, appreciation and understanding of the animal, ballistics, and weaponry; and finely honed skills of patience, tracking and marksmanship.

Fred had matched each animal's greatness and conquered it, for Fred was the proven best of his human kind. Fred and his specimens reached their ultimate pinnacles together. They achieved that unspoken, but understood, profound respect for each other. Fred and every one of his species specimens had proven themselves worthy by coming together with him in the hunt. Each head bore Fred's pride. He harvested only the finest trophy specimen available from every species, thus honoring that species by displaying only the finest example of its kind.

Fred lived his life as if it were the natural extension of his love of blood sport. His opulent mansion had only the finest tapestries, paintings, and sculptures. His magnificently manicured grounds and finest liquors announced that he only tolerated the very best and finest things in life. He now seized upon Marty as the natural compliment to his quest for achievement and recognition. Before she even spoke to him of his bedroom prowess, his mind had begun planning ways to advance his goal of dominance over all other males of his human species.

Miss Shameless recognized success. She expressed her enthusiasm for Marty's smashing breakthrough:

'Girl, he's damn good at this. He's set my vagina on fire, as in I totally loved what he did to me. I want to join my body to his, forever! Tell him how much you loved it. Tell him you want to do more of it. Never let his tongue get away from you! He's a fast learner and he's wonderful. Tell him how much you love him for fucking you

orally like he did. He's a Godsend. Tell him you love him. Let him know you mean it, so he knows. Be honest. Let him know you appreciate him for the man he is. Tell him you love his intimacy.'

"Oh, Fred, you were marvelous. I love how you made me feel. You are soooo good, Fred. You are a true champion! I had such a wild explosive orgasm! I kept coming and coming. I wanted to keep going, Fred. You understood me. You didn't stop! Most men stop, but you didn't! You understood the essential animal inside of me, Fred. You did! You loved me so beautifully, the way you continued kissing my clitoris. My flowing juices were telling you that I love you.

"Could you feel that? Do you like the taste of my love? When you swallowed my love stream, you let me know you completely accepted me and my love. I appreciate that you love me, Fred. It's wonderful to be in love like this. Oh, Fred, my dearest, sweetest love, you made me come twice! When you felt me coming, you held me close to you. You are precious to me. Oh, my dear Fred, you do love me. I feel it. I know you do!"

"Yes, Marty. I do love you," responded an enthusiastic Fred. *"I love you more than all my trophies. I love you more than my wife. I'm crazy in love with you."*

"Our love is so beautiful, Fred. I feel so completely connected to you now." Marty's voice now became its softest, most endearing, earnest and loving.

Marty's hands lifted Fred's face to receive her deep French kisses. She mounted Fred's penis in the lap dance position, again; and wrapped her arms around him. While she kissed him and bathed his cock in her slippery paradise, a transformation of sorts took place in their relationship.

The great hunter was now completely at Marty's mercy. He knew he was about to embark upon a quest of a different sort, a new kind of hunt; a human hunt, which required that he would first become the submissive, captured prey.

No fledgling Puffin or Guillemot chick, confined in its nest, was more helpless to flee its ravishing captor than Fred. His protector wife, like a mother bird away from her nest, was not there to save Fred from Marty's claws. Like a rapacious Black Backed Gull, settled casually on an unprotected nest, unhurriedly tearing apart, and devouring the limbs and bodies of helpless chicks, Marty, now at her undisturbed peaceful leisure, ripped away Fred's heart from its attachment to his wife. Her wistful innocent-seeming eyes stared into Fred's while she swallowed his soul. He enjoyed Marty's dissemblance of his old life and welcomed her opening floodgates to immerse him in his new one.

As her tongue probed Fred's tongue and her confident wanton vagina coaxed renewed life into Fred's cock, Marty knew she was dismembering every facet of Fred's marriage and devouring all affection and fidelity Fred ever felt for his wife. Her eyes smiled into Fred's soul, examining his face for any sign of resistance or flight, much like a bird of prey stands over the nest of helpless chicks, measuring them before devouring them. Fred returned her questioning eyes with an even stronger embrace and deeper kisses. Marty was marauding shamelessly through Fred's marriage vows to his wife, ripping away each covenantal promise he had ever made to her.

Fred did absolutely nothing to resist what was happening. He welcomed all advances from his new found love, his glorious, charming, shameless whore. He drenched his mind in the beauty of Marty's perfectly oval angelic face and lost his thoughts in her dreamy eyes. Her cupid smiling mouth, perky up-lilted nose and deep blue eyes formed the perfect picture of natural innocence.

'*There can not possibly be anything bad about her,*' Fred's mind rationalized his life's transition into Marty's world. '*No woman so beautiful could possibly harbor any hint of evil within her. What we are doing together must have been preordained and fated. Why, her face is the very essence of honest innocence. It is priceless. She's the very essence of innocent vitality. She couldn't possibly harbor a single wicked thought inside a head that beautiful.'*

In Fred's state of mind Marty could have instructed him to bludgeon his wife and bury her body in one of the flower beds. And, he might have done so without questioning her. He was so smitten he would crawl through broken glass to hold her nubile body and kiss her delicious lips, if she would only ask him. He was no longer honoring his wife, nor being faithful to her, not even in any residual sort of way; nor in any sense did he cherish their fidelity bond. He was allowing Marty to tear away and devour every vow he had ever made.

He clasped her luscious lusting body tenderly in his arms; then sliding his surrounding arms up and down over her to better appreciate the awesome fullness of their mutual lust. And he kissed her again and again. The two of them kissed and giggled and teased each other with their touchings while, one by one, Marty casually extinguished every marriage vow ever Fred made, as if they were as insignificant as spent cigarette butts.

"*Do you still promise to honor your wife?*" teased Marty.

"*No, I think I've gone way past that,*" giggled Fred.

"*Do you still promise to cherish your wife all the days of your life?*" whispered Marty into his ear as she stroked his cock, then snuggled her naked body close against his and helped his decision with a soulful French Kiss.

"*I think not,*" whispered a frolic-minded Fred. "*I think I'd rather cherish your tits and your glorious vagina; and the way you release your orgasms into my mouth instead. I'd rather cherish those things, if that's okay with you.*"

"*Well, let me see,*" smiled Marty. She slid down between Fred's thighs, took his cock into her mouth and sucked it to hardness again before she finished her answer. When he was solid and stiff, she lifted herself up to Fred's face. Her dreamy eyes looked into his soul.

"I guess it depends upon whether you still promise to be faithful to your wife all the days of your life? That is a very serious vow, don't you know?" her eyes smiled a coquettish, girlishly innocent, laughing smile with all of lust's immoral abandon her soul could express from within her. She gave her unspoken, personal message to Fred:

'I know you, Fred. I know what you want. I know what you need. You know you need me. You know I'm good for you. You know I'm good for your soul and your self-respect as a man. I know all about you and I love everything about you, too. You are the perfect man for me, too Fred. I adore you, Fred. I'm being completely honest. I love the way you fuck me and I want you to fuck me over and over again. I'll never become tire of fucking you. I'll be everything to you your wife wouldn't even begin to know how to be.'

She resumed stroking Fred's cock while she kissed him and awaited his answer, already knowing he would surely deny his wife.

"To hell with her! She can go fuck herself. You know I can't be faithful to her now that I've fallen in love with you." Fred drew Marty tightly close and returned her kisses. He adored her whoring soul and all the sins she carried within it.

"Fred, darling, has it ever occurred to you that she's probably already fucking herself?" Marty pulled her head back and puckered her lips as if she was revealing the great secret of female masturbation to a choir boy. It was Marty's subtle, effective way of relegating Petunia to Fred's mental trash heap.

He laughed at Marty's inuendo. *"I don't care what she does. I haven't for as long as I can remember; but, answer me this, my glorious gorgeous whore: Can I cherish your tits and vagina?"*

"Oh, Fred, don't be silly. Of course, you can. I'll happily let you fuck me and devour my vagina whenever you can catch me; and that assumes that you will always be very good to me, okay baby?"

"Yes, Marty, a thousand times yes."

"And, Fred, if I'm going to be your girl, I'll need you to understand that I'll have to be notoriously unfaithful to you."

"I'm not possessive." Fred agreed to Marty's open declaration that she would not be tamed or owned. Fred pulled her down on top of him and kissed her fully on the mouth. In this manner, their bargain was struck. Marty would become a regular consort for Fred. She would be the dazzling trophy that enhanced his image amongst his fellow hunter friends. She would constantly flatter his ego and patronize his image of himself, all the while pouring poison into his ear about the drabness and inadequacies of his wife.

In return he would lavish money and gifts upon her. Marty intuited that Fred's wife would be relegated to the dust bin of his life, resigned to spend her days in Florida playing Mahjong with her aging mommy; trying not to think about the things Marty was doing with her husband; trying not to think about what was happening to her shattered marriage and her life.

That day was all sport play for Marty. She thoroughly enjoyed watching Fred laugh and smile while she joked about Petunia's meekness and mocked her marriage. She purred contentedly while stroking Fred's cock and trampling his marriage to rubble. Fred understood exactly what Marty was doing. He cared for Marty all right, but in his own self-aggrandizing sort of way.

He understood his new relationship with Marty left no room for Petunia. He would be ditching her like he would be putting down an old, faithful companion dog. But he had fallen in love with the idea that Marty was taking the old mutt's place in his bed. He held the vivacious, innocent looking whore even closer and kissed her mouth with more passion than he ever had before, anticipating more nights like tonight in his future. He offered no resistance whatsoever to this iniquitous shameless woman; only his approval of her tactics; his adoration of and acquiescence to her immoral whoring.

Fred's passion for trophy quests never relented. He was hard wired that way. In the months ahead he would take measures to ensure that Marty, his trophy whore, would recognize his unparalleled ability to meet her in her habitat and assert his dominance over her. At the same time, he would ensure that every person in his world and beyond recognized that he had bagged her as his personal trophy.

He would first enlarge his personal charitable foundation from thirty-five million to a hundred million; replace Petunia as his co-director and install Marty in that position with a salary of twenty thousand dollars a month. The foundation would purchase a new Ferrari convertible and membership in a private jet transportation service for Marty's exclusive use. He would then incorporate a film production company to finance and co-produce ten high end porn films using premium world class settings and name recognizable movie actors and sports stars as Marty's porn partners.

Each film would have a trailer that prominently displayed Fred's name as the co-producer, thus ensuring that all males would know that Marty was his personal trophy. He would hire a publicist to advertise her films, with his name on the advertising slicks as the films' producer. In this way, the entire world would see Fred as the ultimate winner of the world's most highly prized female specimen, the planet's most exquisite, most perfectly formed, most beautiful, completely immoral whore. Fred and Marty would have a lucrative, long-lasting future relationship and unique understanding, together.

While in the present, Marty was enjoying herself. She was feeling her glorious, promiscuous best. She chortled her pleasures at Fred's complicity with her destruction of Petunia by pushing her lap dancing belly hard against Fred's, as if to cement their co- conspiracy with Marty's heartfelt, ardent, seemingly endless coitus. She thrusted her pelvis against Fred's cock ever harder and faster now, in furiously crazed abandon.

Her moral essence had become much like that of a rapacious gull's: frenzy ripping away at the wings and legs of her helpless victims, casually murdering them; then remorselessly swallowing their body parts down her insatiable gullet of wanton sin. But Marty's feasting was not upon the limbs of helpless young birds; rather she dined gluttonously upon Fred's dismembered feelings for his wife. Her eyes danced with gleeful pleasure while her belly laughs chortled with pleasure over her latest conquest.

She threw her head back and opened her shameless vice savoring mouth to sigh. It was the perfect time for a triumphant interlude. After clawing the guts out of Fred's marriage and filling her stomach with the essence of Fred's connubial past, Marty needed to pause from her exertions. She had figuratively transformed Fred's wife from a viable loving spouse into a nuisance to him; a useless shredded repulsive carcass that dragged down his image. It was time to toss Petunia from her nest like the worthless gutted, plucked, and picked over heap that she was.

Relaxed from her conquest, Marty resumed love making; but now more lovingly and slowly. She was completely relaxed. The tensions of conquest had passed and she could concentrate on her body pleasures without other thoughts. She loved feeling a cock inside her, pleasuring her slowly. She placed her hands about Fred's neck and whispered her promises of love to him, not unlike a gull lifting its prey morsel high up to assure itself of the worthiness of its prize before downing it into its gullet.

Her sweet whispers swallowed every remaining trace scrap of Fred's marital fidelity. She had severed Fred's heart from its spousal passions, and his soul from its matrimonial loyalty, like an experienced beak casually rips limbs from a chick's body.

Her eyes held Fred's gaze. This was Marty's way to cement her man's soul to hers, and make him crazy for her approval and love. They looked into Fred's eyes and captured back the love he was sending her. His eyes craved her warmth and her bodily closeness. Her eyes took in the love that he sent her way and held it close to her heart. When she saw love in a man's eyes this way, it meant something profound to her. Marty lived for that something. Then, she did what was only natural for her. She fondled that love with her own eyes, caressed it as she held a long, appreciating blink; kissed it with silent meaning in her eyes and sent it back to Fred's eyes, replying to the understanding message he had conveyed:

'I'll love you like no other woman has ever loved you. I'm a very loving woman. I'll be everything you can imagine a lover can be. You'll see. The more we make love, the more you'll know my love for you is for real.'

Those sacred vow lines that had once moored Fred and his marriage partner to their safe anchorages were now irreparably severed. Like a ship adrift in a troubled ocean, Fred's passion and spirit for his Petunia was suddenly vulnerable to Marty's storm-tossed sea. Marital love's stay-lines were snaped by Marty's rapacious waves of lust. Marriage, their once reliable anchor, lay useless on the sea floor. The passion and spirit of Fred's and Petunia's united life was doomed to a losing struggle against the whims of Marty's pleasure. Fred knew his feelings for Petunia could no longer survive. They were engulfed and swallowed beneath Marty's lust waves.

But those tender passions did not simply disappear and go away, just as sunken ships and devoured body parts do not simply go away. Fred's passions and spirit for marital fidelity became Marty's new possessions. She salvaged them like the discoverer of a wreck claims its spoils. The tender feelings Fred once carried for Petunia, he now carried for Marty. He was head over heels, blindly in love with his shameless whore; without second thoughts, doubts, or reservations.

Like body parts of Puffins and other such innocents slide into a gull's gullet, sustaining it, Fred's newly devoured marriage would sustain Marty for a time; and renew the certainty of her immoral convictions. But one meal does not suffice forever. Marty knew she'd move on to raid other marriage nests. She knew she would need to feast again, and again, and again.

'Now pander to him, stroke his ego. Tell him how great he was. That will steady him and allow you to put your saddle on him. Then, point the direction you want him to go and ride him anywhere.' Miss Shameless had her way of keeping Marty clear headed about her role as a seductress.

"Fred, my love, we must do this often. I've never felt this close to anyone before. I've never been loved so sweetly and completely. You are my champion. You have conquered my heart. You are my source of pride. I am so proud of you. I'm so thrilled that you are unafraid to be with me. Have you any idea how much that means to me? How much that lifts me up? Can you possibly know how much that makes me respect you and love you more than I could ever love anyone? I want us to make love whenever we can be together. I want to feel you conquering me, pulsing your sweet cream into me, again and again!"

'You've done it!' Miss Iniquity congratulated her. *'His wife's ears will never hear his tongue tell her how it yearns for its newly acquired taste. Her skin will never feel the pleasures of his hands touching her everywhere, and rubbing her with exotic oils. She will never experience the new ways he has learned to give a woman's sex*

its sweet oral pleasures. And, her mind will never again sleep joined to the same thoughts as his.

'But his tongue will often crave to slake its thirst in YOUR delicious lusts; his hands will yearn to explore every inch of YOU, again and again; and his cock will throb with desire to revisit the pleasures inside YOUR mouth and vagina. And, his dreams will keep him wrapped in YOUR arms; and no longer in his wife's. Congratulations! You've conquered your conqueror!'

Her own thoughts confirmed Iniquity's opinion.

'I felt his mind accept me. Tranquility comes over a lover when he's certain his woman loves him. Fred is there. I'm certain our bond is solid. My sex is firmly embedded in every cranny of his limbic zone. I will wean him further away from Petunia and tie him ever closer to me.'

Over the following months, Marty strengthened her grip on Fred's mind. She convinced him that the blissful happiness of his splendid cock, and the enhancement of his manly image were her life's primary mission.

Petunia's bridge clubs, travel outings and visits to her mommy soon became meaningless trivialities in Fred's eyes. Marty made sure of that. She mocked, scoffed, sneered, and laughed at Petunia's pursuits. She methodically wiped away Fred's interest in his wife and everything the woman held dear. She removed Petunia from Fred's mind, like one wipes lifeless dust away from furniture to restore its luster.

"*Fred, darling,*" teased Marty during a languid afternoon of love making, "*Has Petunia ever mentioned that your left testicle twirls faster than your right testicle?*" Her eyes were their teasing best. She had been mouthing Fred's balls, first one then the other, while exquisitely performing her sensuous fellatio. Fred was fully erect. Marty's slavish attention to every sensory receptor along the shaft and head of her penis friend noticed the anomaly. She had licked its length, tooth tickled its length, tongue kissed and suckled its head and foreskin; and had just finished mouthing its balls, first its left testicle, then its right one.

"My wife has never had her mouth anywhere near my cock. I thought you knew that," Fred's eyes were questioning.

"Oh, that's right, you did tell me that," Marty's slight pout feigned forgetfulness for her lapse of memory. *"I guess I forgot. I guess I just love sucking you and playing mouth games with your penis so much that I couldn't actually let myself believe she wouldn't love doing that, too."*

Marty smiled a devilish smile as she kissed Fred's mouth. Her kiss delivered an intimate mental sensation, completing the limbic zone's connection of Fred's mind to his penis. Her casual shamelessness was the magical bond between them. She was performing her seduction art at her witty, teasing best. She laid her head on the pillow, facing him. Her hair maintained its freshly washed curl, gracing her child-like innocent face. She was stunning; beautiful. Her lips delivered soft kisses to his while her hand continued massaging his testicles.

"Your balls fascinate me. I love holding them in my hands. I like feeling them rolling over and over, making more semen for me. I love them, Fred. Promise me they're mine, forever."

"They're yours, forever, you gorgeous, shameless whore." Fred gave her an assuring smile.

"Good. Now I know they're really busy, making more semen; all for me. I'm very proud of them." Marty purred. *"I could play with them for hours. I love how relaxed and pleased you are while I play with them. All your cares seem to evaporate. I feel wonderful, seeing you happy like this, Fred."*

Marty was unassuming, uncaring, unapologetically louche. Sexuality was the natural, unconventional way of life for her. It was her matter-of-fact way of blending entertainment and exploration with her alternative, proudly immoral lifestyle. She lived unrestrained by thoughts or boundaries. Nothing confined her. No subject was taboo. Her erotic pleasure world was a magical, ethereal, creative place.

Her thoughts easily slipped into and were embraced within mysterious workings of the limbic zones of her lovers. She played with their minds in debauched provocative ways, while her body's hands, lips, tongue, and vagina simultaneously played Eros with their sensualities. She was unique among women in the way she wove her uninhibited naturalness into her dalliances. She was a whore exemplar, extraordinaire; and incredibly beautiful and lovable. The theater where she put on her magnificent, innocent appearing performances was the bedroom.

PETUNIA PURGED

"Fred, darling," She cooed in his ear, *"something is troubling me and I feel I should mention it."* She understood both of Fred's minds well enough to know that this day, this moment, was her opportune time. Her hand continued massaging Fred's balls.

"What's troubling you, sweetheart?" Fred's question was the unconcerned sort, as if he expected her to ask him which restaurant they should choose for a late dinner. It confirmed his mood. After an hour of Marty's delightful cock teasing, he was eminently pliable.

"Well, Fred," she shifted her position so her eyes could lovingly stare into the innermost workings of his mind. *"Sometimes I have this creepy sense while I'm staying with you and making love here in your bedroom. I suspect Petunia's spirit is watching us and trying to make me feel guilty for loving you so much. I know it's silly, but it's a terrible feeling. I'm afraid she'll break in here while we're making love. I'd hate to have a terrible scene, Fred. I*

don't want her bothering us. My sense frightens me. I want you to make it go away."

Marty waited for Fred's reply. She knew better than to push for an answer. The master hunter would be more manly if he offered the solution to her distress. She waited for Fred to take the bait. Fred understood immediately what Marty required of him. He had observed times when cheetahs, cougars and lions sometimes brought down their prey animal; when they even had its neck in their death grip; but the victim animal put on a sudden adrenalin burst of strength and will; and it wrested itself free and escaped. Marty was no fool. She knew she had knocked Petunia down. She knew she held Fred's wife's fate in her death grip.

But unlike an inexperienced or uncertain predator cat, Marty knew what made a kill complete. She knew she needed to keep her kill down. Petunia could not be allowed to escape her death grasp. Fred sensed what Marty wanted; or rather what she did not want. She did not want Petunia to burst into their bedroom, making a scene. Marty did not want an indignant wife screaming and throwing Marty's scents and make up at her or at a wall; or ordering Marty to leave *her* bedroom. Marty did not want to be in a situation where Petunia could stand on moral high ground and order Marty out of *her* house. Fred knew Marty now needed his help to secure her kill.

"Sweetheart, how can I help you with this? Make the arrangements, whatever you like, and I'll authorize them." Fred took her into his arms and pulled her close to him. He'd swallowed the bait whole because he wanted to before she even asked. Marty sensed that he'd agree to all the changes she was about to suggest. She kissed him with her most soulful French kiss, promising him a huge reward for allowing her to expunge his wife's demon spirit from her life.

The following day Fred signed paperwork needed to affect Marty's desired changes. Over the ensuing two weeks they were put into effect. The locks to the estate's gates and all its buildings were changed. Only Fred and Marty had keys. Key codes to the garage access were also changed. Only Fred and Marty had the new key codes. Fred's wife's request for a new set of keys and codes was denied. Petunia's authorizations on her credit and debit cards, expense accounts, brokerage accounts and bank accounts were cancelled; and new authorizations were issued to Marty.

Petunia's household possessions, clothes, toiletries, and jewelry were carted away and given to charities; and the mansion's master bedroom, where Marty plied her seductions, was completely remodeled. A new California king sized bed with new Giza cotton bedding, and a surfeit of new pillows replaced all the old bedding. Erotic tapestries of nymphs enjoying their love making were hung on the walls. Petunia's pastoral art pictures were unceremoniously trashed. New bedroom furniture, featuring erotic oriental soapstone and jade figures in provocative suggestive positions replaced the old dressers. The drawers of the new furniture pieces now stored Marty's erotic lingerie, her assorted vibrators, and accessories for performing BDSM. Her walk-in wardrobe sported dozens of newly acquired designer dresses, coats, furs, and shoes. Her private bathroom now contained her personalized blends of perfumes, toiletry scents, and soaps. Petunia's store-bought fragrances were trashed.

After making love in the remodeled bedroom, Marty reflected on her achievement. Petunia's efforts to thwart her ambition had always been feeble, ineffective; even laughable. Her sobs and furtive phone calls to her social friends went unheeded. Petunia's friends feared provoking a fight with Fred. They decided not to interfere. Fred was Marty's now. The ruthlessness she displayed while devastating her mousy rival was only exceeded by her wantonness. Lying atop Fred, shrouding him in her silken hair and smiling into his eyes with her child-like innocent face, she sharing with him the marvelous thrill she experienced from his latest ejaculation. As her sex squirmed while nestled over his sated penis, she felt a glorious inner pride. She had reconfirmed who she was and what of what destructions she was capable. She had destroyed not just any hapless woman, like Carl's wife; but Fred's wife, a woman of very high social standing.

By combining her inimitable seduction craft, intoxicating shamelessness, and psychologically intriguing perspectives about the glories of immorality, she had expeditiously displaced a woman nearly twice her age; and dispatched her to her mommy. Marty's eyes smiled her deeply felt satisfaction. Her lips parted and her cheeks broadened the delights that glowed in her face. Before she would take Fred's neck and lift his head to her lips, before she would French kiss him again to signal her appreciation for his love and commitment to her, she took a brief internal inventory of herself.

Marty knew herself. She accepted that she was an immoral, self-aggrandizing, pleasure-seeking whore. She harbored no doubts that she was stunningly attractive, shamelessly sensual, and magnificent in her sexual crafts. With Fred, she demonstrated to herself that her whore craft had advanced to a new, higher plateau. Her game was played far above common streetwalkers' sex-for-money transaction levels. She congratulated herself:

'By studying Fred and appreciating his need for ego recognition, I captured his affections and made him fall in love with me; on my terms. By appealing to his sense of manliness I ran off his wife and ensconced myself in his bedroom; remodeled in a sensuous, erotica theme; more to my liking. By next making Fred the envy of his male friends, I intend to legitimize and expand my predatory conduct.'

Marty schemed to broaden her horizons into Fred's social world. The women and the men in that crowd behaved like they were an impenetrable snobbish clique. She reckoned that none of these women would ever invite her to one of their parties or social functions. That would alienate the others in their group. They were older, but their behaviors much mirrored the behaviors of the WEX girls and their parents.

Breaking into their social circle required an innovative approach. She needed some way to make known her availability to the male members of their clique. After that hurdle was overcome, Marty figured that the phone calls would come; the barriers to her promiscuity would fall and more clandestine romantic affairs would follow.

The men of the group talked and gossiped about hunting, politics, and women. Word of Marty's availability and charms would surely circulate. One by one, she would pry loose each woman's hold on her man. For Marty, hunting these hunters would be like shooting fish in a barrel.

Petunia never expected there could ever be such a rapid collapse of her world. She underestimated the powers of a willful whore. Marty blindsided her. In the blink of an eye, Fred's wife found herself proscribed from her own home, her credit and checking accounts, her perfectly ordered social world, her assets and many of her personal possessions. She discovered herself exiled from the life she'd cultivated, nurtured, and enjoyed. Her once steady, reliable husband now treated her like an undesirable criminal. She had nowhere to go; and no immediate money. She hastily retreated to Florida and her new, lower status world of Mommy and Mahjong.

After another month passed, Marty's muted sniffles ensured that Fred would intuit that something was not well with their relationship. He would know that his dream mistress was troubled.

She sat upright in bed in this early morning hour. The sun's rays streaked through one of the room's stained-glass windows, adding luster and warmth as it danced in her hair. Her eyes looked melancholy and despairing. She personified feminine helplessness and nature's godsend of innocence.

"Marty, darling, what's wrong? Have you been crying? Tell me, sweetheart." Fred, for all his manly huntsman image, had a soft spot for Marty's feelings and needs. Love does that to a man. His inner alarm told him there was something he needed to make right. The love of his life must never feel distressed. His manliness told him he needed to do something. Seeing sadness in the eyes of his lover was intolerable.

"Oh, Fred," Marty turned to him. Her eyes were pools of deep perplexity; her face was masked in forlorn helplessness. She hugged him tightly; her eyes stared her most distant wonder look at the ceiling. She took his hands and held them in hers for a long silent moment before she spoke. *"I've had a terrible dream. It made me wake up feeling ashamed of myself. I don't know how to tell you about it, but I can not live with the thought of it and how it made me feel. It was terrible; and it's awkward for me to talk about it."*

"Try me, baby. I want you to be happy." His voice was sincere, as if in confidence with a child. *"What dream did that bad sandman bring you? Perhaps I can fix it."* Fred, always the understanding gentleman, looked at her with questioning puppy dog eyes. Plainly, he loved her unconditionally.

"Oh, Fred, it was so awful," she wailed, allowing a fearful expression to color her words. *"You got mad at me; and you even called me a whore in a nasty kind of way, sniff, sniff."* She wiped tears away from her eyes.

"I felt terrible, Fred. Then, I woke up and I started thinking. I said to myself: 'Maybe Fred really does think of me as his whore, and not as his lover. Maybe Fred really thinks he's too good for me, like I could

never be his equal,' She sniffed her nose and wiped away a tear. *"And then my mind started doing what it does to me, Fred. It started asking me why I didn't feel like your equal. So, I've been sitting here feeling sorry for myself. I've been thinking that no matter how many erotic films I make I'll probably never have as much money as you and I'll never feel like your true equal. And, Fred, it's all because of money. That's so terrible, Fred because I know I love you and it's not because of your money that I love you. It's because of the man you are. But I don't know what I can do about it. Can you understand?"*

Her doe eyes pleaded with his heart. She needed to hear him say he understood.

"Yes, I guess I do understand. I'm terribly sorry, sweetheart. Money should never come between us as lovers, never!" Fred shook his head to emphasize his disdain for their inequality in the money department. *"What do you suppose we can do about it?"*

"Well, sweet love," Marty purred as she ran her finger delicately down Fred's nose to touch his lips, then his chin, *"I suppose we could try just one time to let me know how it feels to have some real money of my own. I mean the credit cards and the car and all the things you buy me are wonderful; and I'm deeply grateful and all; but what I'm wishing I could feel is that knowing feeling; that you accept me unconditionally in my own right as a woman of means on my own; and that we love each other because we respect and love each other, not that I............"*

Fred cut her off. *"Stop it, Marty. I don't ever want you to feel like you need to beg me for anything. You don't. I love you. You know I love you. So, let's clear this up right now. I'm going to give you three million dollars. That makes you a woman of means, so you need not concern yourself that you're some kind of toy of mine because you need my money; or that I use my money to control you. I want you feeling as free as a bird. I want your love only because you want to give it, not because you give it for money, okay?"*

Marty didn't say a word. Her eyes smiled and her head nodded, saying it all. Her finger traveled lower; and lower until it found its way past Fred's chest and stomach to his cock. There, Marty joined it with its other digital friends and mouth. Fred and his cock had a wonderful fellatio wake up.

'I really love this arrangement,' thought Marty. *'I'll use that money to buy more promotional spots for my erotic films; and that will make me more money. I'll even co- produce some of my upcoming films, especially the ones with Marshawn, and eventually I'll start my own production company. That will help me get noticed more than I am already. My new films will titillate Fred into an erotic frenzy over me. Fred will love me even more. I'm sure he'll give me more millions; and then I'll promote myself more until I'll soon be desired by the wealthiest billionaires and top movie stars. Being Fred's lover makes for a great trade. He's a keeper, no matter how many more lovers I eventually have.'*

Marty reconfirmed what her mother's behavior and her own experience had already proven without leaving any room for doubt.

'The way to a man's heart and his wealth is not thorough his stomach or his mind. That is old fashioned Victorian nonsense. There is but one path to travel if a woman wants to embed herself in a man's heart and his wallet. It's the same time-honored marvelous road that knowing seductresses have discovered since time immemorial: It's the Penis Pleasure Parkway.'

Marty expected Fred would eventually make his first social appearance with her. She knew the two of them would create a sensational scandal, especially because of the way she would plan it. Petunia's retreat to Florida would be the gossip of the town for weeks. From Florida, Petunia would nurse her wounded pride, make futile calls to her lifelong social friends, and grieve over her shattered marriage. Her image as a loser would sink her credibility into the social mud, while Fred's manly self image would sky-rocket. Marty correctly calculated that, after her smashing debut as femme fatale, she would thereafter accompany Fred to every major social event in the city.

TALK

Fred had bought Marty her new Ferrari convertible which she kept at his garage. This flashy reward for her whoring lifted her notoriety to a higher level, only shared by movie stars. Gossips were mentioning her name with greater frequency. Men silently wondered what she was all about. Fred's friends had spotted them together. They remarked about her to each other:

First male gossip: *"Have you seen the babe that's been hanging with Fred?"*

Second male gossip: *"Yeah, a real looker, I've seen her; she's gorgeous. What's going on with Fred?"*

First male gossip: *"Gorgeous! Shit, man, she's the most beautiful woman I've ever seen. That face! That body! Sweet Jesus, she makes my cock hard. I've seen her in a thin sweater without a bra. Her tits tilt up and her nipples stick out like little cherries. I've never seen a woman with a more beautiful rack. And, that ass of hers is to die for. I saw it fill out her tight shorts. I couldn't take my eyes off it. My mouth started watering. She's out of this world. I checked her out. Wait for it.! Wait for it!*

"She's a fucking porn star! I couldn't believe it. She's a fuck your brains out, fucking porn star! I asked myself: Why would a woman who is that beautiful be making porn films? Why isn't she a movie actress? She'd be a box office sensation.

"The only thing that explains it is that she must love to fuck. I mean, like she must be totally obsessed with fucking. What else could it be? I've watched her on film. I've tried to get into her head. Then it dawned on me. Maybe she makes more money being a top porn star than being a movie actress? Maybe she's mastered the expressions of intimacy's beauty and turned porn into a high brow art form? Her mind must be thinking along those lines. That's the only thing that explains it. By her way of thinking, her work isn't porn. It's art."

Second male gossip: *"I have a hard time believing Fred is fucking her. She can't even be half his age. Can you believe Fred is fucking that? He must have ditched Petunia for her. I had to check out a couple of her films. Man, oh man, does she ever love to fuck and suck! I mean, she puts my heart in my throat. She totally loves fucking; working a cock with her cunt; and it shows. She loves her work. I can't imagine Fred keeping up with her.*

"I've never seen a woman who is so expressive while she's fucking. There's a certain happiness about her while she's doing it. She totally loves it. I mean, she sometimes fucks non-stop, like she's a wild crazy mink, and then other times she fucks so fucking sweetly you just can't help falling in love with her. I mean like obsessing over her. She's happy about what she's doing the entire time. Not shy. Not guilty. Not unsure about herself. Just happy; joyous. She's wonderful and beautiful. It's like you want to hold her in your arms and take her home to Momma. I get a monster hard-on from watching her. I'd love to get into her panties. Hell, I'd plant my face in her vagina if she'd let me. She's unbelievable."

First male gossip: *"Somebody told me she works at Sustack's. So, what does that make her? Is she an investment rep or a porn star?"*

Second male gossip: *"Don't know the answer to that, maybe both. Her name is Marty. Maybe she fucks for business, maybe Sustack's is just a front for her porn business. I've heard weird things about Sustack's since old Marvin died. Susan Mallory was Marvin's whore. That woman has more money than God. She owns six skyscrapers in downtown. She's still there. She still does tricks for their big pension clients; and this Marty, who sees Fred, is Susan's daughter. Hooking must run in that family. That place has a shady reputation, so you may want to do some checking, find out what you're getting into, before you hit on her. I've heard that some people who worked with Sustack somehow disappear."*

First male gossip: *"Don't believe everything you hear. They're a regulated company, lots of audits and stuff. Maybe they just tell people to leave quietly. Maybe there are signed confidentiality agreements and people just go away. Who knows? But, hey! If you find out about her deal with Fred, let me know. If I find out anything I'll tell you. Maybe she'll do a two for one."*

Second male gossip: *"Fred's got serious money. He bought her a fucking Ferrari. So, I think you're delusional if you think she'll fuck the two of us for a dinner and a few hundred bucks."*

First male gossip: *"A Ferrari? No shit?"*

Second male gossip: *"No shit! That's pocket change for Fred. That should make you think we've got zero chance."*

First male gossip: *"Don't know, about that. I didn't say there's no chance. There's always a chance. After all, a whore's a whore. We just don't know enough to know what it takes to have time with her. Let's stay in touch. Let me know if you hear anything."*

Second male gossip: *"Okay."*

Fred's friends were bursting with curiosity. Why, they wondered, did Fred buy that woman a Ferrari? What was it about her that charmed him so? She seemed aloof, exclusive, yet somehow inviting and accessible. Their imaginations played mind games with them. They wanted to discover her for themselves. Marty created a stir in the male organization.

MARRIAGE TRAP

Later that decisive afternoon, when Marty lap straddled Fred yet again, and after he ejaculated inside her a third time, he told her he loved her and that he wanted to *marry* her. Marty knew that her love making could sometimes have that effect on a man. She understood she had Fred ensnared. He was as securely hers as a fish that had swallowed a bait hook. Her intimacy barbs were deeply imbedded in his guts. He couldn't shake himself free of her now, even if he wanted to. It was too late for that. He trusted her now. But he didn't want to break free. That thought never crossed his mind. The only thoughts he had were how badly he needed her, and how much he loved her. *And,* he was addicted to her love making. Marty controlled his feelings now. Slowly, she began reeling him in.

Miss Iniquity understood the situation perfectly. She knew it was time to step in. She whispered:

'*Be careful about matrimony talk, girl. Avoid getting into a legal tiff with his wife before you've got his money. Remember, this is about money. Give him some slack when he tries to control you; but don't let him throw your hook. Make him continue paying to play. You know you're not the marrying kind of girl, anyway.*'

"*Oh, Fred, a respectable country gentleman like you shouldn't rush into marriage with a shameless whore like me,*" Marty whispered demurely in a low-pitched voice while lovingly stroking his cock with her fingers. "*I have a terrible reputation, Fred. I'm known as an incorrigible, shameless whore. You already know that about me. I love to play and I love being a very bad girl. Why, I could leave you for weeks at a time to run off to the other side of the world to have fun somewhere. As much as I do love you Fred, I honestly can't help myself from being naughty. It's so hard for me to say no,*" she purred while softly rubbing his chest.

"*Some women like to work in an office all day or be at home with their kids. But, I'm not like those women, Fred. I love being naughty. I love being invited into other women's bedrooms, Fred. It makes me feel like, you know, a top predator; like I can't be tamed like all those other women. You already know how much I love sex, Fred.*

"And, I have terrible morals, Fred. I'm as immoral and naughty as any girl can be. Tee Hee. I'm often interviewed by WORLD INTI-MACY BEAT, the live TV channel that's owned by INTIMATE ARTISTRY PERFORMANCE MAGAZINE. In my last interview with Consuelo Lovely, I explained why I'm a devotee of the Modern Morality Standard; which means I don't have any morals at all. You should watch that interview on the internet before you decide to get serious about me, Fred.

"You need to know all these naughty things people say about me, Fred; I'm a shameless pleasure seeker. I freely admit I love sex and I don't care who knows it. I'm a believer in the ancient pagan tra-ditions that were practiced before the Near Eastern and European tribes were conquered by those nasty Romans; and then by those righteous Christians, with their concepts of morality and misguided notions about the sins of female adultery. My soul wants to live in those uncomplicated, more honest times when men worshipped the female vagina as the source of creation; when they felt it was a sacred rite to kiss the vagina, honor it and copulate with it. I believe those pagan rites were the innocent, honest way of life.

"I'm the woman I am, Fred. I'll always crave the initial pene-tration of a new partner's penis. I'll always be curious about mak-ing love with a new lover. It's always an exciting and beautiful experience for me. It's the nymphomania that lives within me. I can't escape from it and I don't want to, either. It's an adorable feeling. I love it. I feel no shame in it. I can't help how I feel. I love the variety and the sex. I don't try to hide it, either. I flaunt it. I promote it. When I have a new lover's penis inside me, I desper-ately want to convert him to my New Morality Standard ways of thinking and living. I am so excited for him and his penis. I just want to fuck and fuck and fuck until I've fucked the life out of both

of us. And I smile my most glorious smile. My face becomes the poster girl face of immorality.

"And I see myself as a Pagan Goddess from twenty thousand years ago. I imagine my spirit voices are guiding me; telling me how glorious and ravishing I am. They are congratulating me while I achieve my intimate bonding with my new lover. And, Fred, I have these flashbacks to when I was a Pagan Temple prostitute of twenty thousand years ago. I can vividly see myself murdering my new lover's wife; hacking her body to pieces and eviscerating her; even eating her heart and liver, symbolizing that I have devoured every trace of her spirit and taken her man as my own. He no longer has any need of her. He becomes completely mine."

"Marty," Fred adjusted his position on the bed and peered deeply into her eyes. For the first time, he recognized there were no limits to her demonic desires. *"Hypothetically speaking, would you like to have me tie up Petunia and watch you while you eviscerate her and eat her heart and liver?"*

"Oh Fred, my dearest, sweetest love, would you really consider doing that for me? Would you like to assist me while I murder your wife?"

"Well, hypothetically speaking, yes, I would. I suppose there is historical precedence for this sort of thing, if we could view it as a ritual cleansing sort of process."

"Ritual cleansing? In what way, darling?"

"Well, the ancient Hebrews had a ceremony where they placed all their sins onto the head of a goat. Then they led the goat over a cliff face and it plunged to its death, taking all the sins of the tribe with it."

"Oh! The scapegoat!"

"Yes, exactly. Then the Christians modified the ceremony and made their Christ the scapegoat. When Christians eat their wafer host and drink their wine, they are symbolically eating the body and

drinking the blood of their Christ. He is dying for their sins, assuming the historic tribal role of scapegoat."

"Yes. So, do you think, perhaps, that my flashbacks to twenty thousand years ago are similar? Do you think my spirit soul predates the Hebrew scapegoating ritual? Is it possible that I really was a Temple Priestess Prostitute? Is it possible that my spirit soul relives some ancient ritual where I eviscerate my rival and devour her inner essence? I mean, back then, the heart and liver were considered the dwellings of the spirit soul, not the brain. Back then we humans didn't have any appreciation for our brains. We didn't even know what our brains did or why we had them."

"Possibly. Marty, darling, you may carry the reincarnation of a Pagan Goddess spirit soul. Your flashbacks may be a way of expressing your inner feelings of triumph. The flashbacks may be your way of forgiving yourself for murdering your rival's lifestyle; for taking her marriage from her. It may be your way of putting the entire episode behind you and moving forward. It's your personal form of scapegoating; and it predates the Hebrew practice."

"Then, there's nothing wrong with me for feeling this way? There's nothing wrong with me feeling I want to eviscerate Petunia and eat her heart and liver?"

No, love, I don't think there is anything wrong with your for having those desires. It seems based on early human practices and it's perfectly normal. But in our time, it would be illegal and punishable by death. As much as I'd love to watch you doing that to Petunia, I'd never forgive myself if the authorities found you out. They would take you away from me, forever. And I cannot allow that. I have a better idea."

"What, love? Please tell me." Marty looked dreamily into Fred's eyes and gently stroked his penis.

"Well, we can do something similar to what the ancient Hebrews did. We can use a substitute victim for Petunia. The next time I

kill a moose, elk, antelope, buffalo, or deer, we will have our own private ritual. I'll have it eviscerated for you and its heart and liver removed. We'll pretend its organs are Petunia's and we will say a prayer over them. And then I will cook them up for us and we will eat them. And as we eat them, we will know that we are devouring the spirit soul of Petunia and condemning her to our past, forever. Would that work for you, darling?"

"Yes. That would be lovely. But there would need to be one additional thing."

"What would that be, love?"

"After our ritual dinner, I'll want to relive my spirit soul's experience of twenty thousand years ago. I'll be filled with desire. I'll want to make love with Petunia's husband that whole night. I'll want to make love until we both pass out from exhaustion. Could we do that, Fred, my daring?"

"Of course!" Fred ginned broadly. *"I'd enjoy that immensely; and I'd rather expect nothing less from my Temple Goddess."*

"Oh, thank you, my love." Marty began kissing the head of Fred's penis. *"I'm so happy that you understand me. You have no idea how much that means to me, Fred. You understand that I have the soul of a Pagan Temple Prostitute. You know how much I love to fuck; and you know how I cannot stand the thought of any other woman being more important than me."*

"Yes, I understand you, darling; and I love you. I know your essence as the most highly prized specimen of all things feminine. You are my ultimate prize. I adore you. You know I adore you. You have captured my heart."

"I appreciate that, Fred. And I also need you to understand that, no matter what I do or who I am with, your love is the one love that captures me and holds me. It's because you understand me. I know that some narrow-minded people have labeled me a slut, Fred; so, when we're out together you might hear ditchwater words spoken

about me. People can be derogatory and demeaning. They may also try to demean the beautiful artistry of my films. But if we're going to be serious about each other; and often be seen together, you can expect small minded people will talk about us."

"Ha," Fred chuckled, "I never pay attention to small minded people."

"I'm so thrilled to hear you say that, darling; because I won't stop my film productions because of gossips. Intimate artistry is my chosen career. I'm proud of my work. I work very hard to perfect every aspect of it. I'm driven to be the best performer in my field. And I love feeling free and uninhibited in my sexuality. I think of myself as a performing artist who specializes in explicit erotica films. I love dressing sexily. I love being noticed. And, I absolutely love getting naked; being fondled, and stimulated while making my adult films, Fred. It doesn't embarrass me in the slightest to perform. Performing lifts my ego and my sense of being a superior, desirable woman. I believe intimacy films are the world's most expressive art genre. They are beautiful and they lift the human spirit. That's why more and more, people are appreciating the beauty of pornography. I crave freely expressing my pleasures while I'm having sex; and I feel thrills while expressing my orgasms in front of the cameras. I emphasize the beauty of human intimacy. It's the ultimate expressive human feeling. It's what I do so wonderfully; and its who I am, Fred.

"I love exploring different sex positions with my newest partners while I'm making my films, Fred; and I salivate at every opportunity to perform orgy scenes on camera. My lusts overwhelm me when several men have me at once. I love staring in orgy themed films. They help me bring out my expressive best. They are like laboratories where I can get immediate feedback while I vary my techniques with different partners. And then, my love, I can be the very best of myself with you. Please understand me, my darling. I must constantly challenge myself to be the best porn star I can possibly be. I try very hard

to be that ultimate woman, that most sought trophy you want for your very own. It's my way of expressing my love for you, Fred.

"But you mentioned marriage. I want you to hold that thought, Fred. Can you imagine how everyone would talk about you if we got engaged or married, Fred? Many people are terribly narrow-minded. They would never understand how deeply we love each other. They'd even refuse to believe us when we tell them we're in love. They only want to see you as a man who's taken up with a notoriously immoral woman.

"Think, Fred. What do you think people will say about YOU if they saw ME on your arm? I think they would see that we have become an 'item.' I think they would immediately understand that I've fallen head over heels in love with you. Then I think they'd ask themselves what a distinguished man like YOU could possibly want with a naughty sin-loving, promiscuous girl like ME. Why, they'd probably think you've changed your whole life-style! Likely, they'd also see you as a lady killer, Fred; the man who bagged the world's most beautiful porn star. But, Fred, would you really want the stigma of having a notorious porn star as your wife? Then, people would talk behind your back, but in a different, derogatory sort of way. Do you really want that? Wouldn't it be better for your image if we were just seen as an' item?' That's more mysterious and intriguing, don't you think? People would wonder how you conquered me."

Fred stared at her, as if perplexed, wondering if Marty was trying to ditch him before their romance had barely begun. A long thirty seconds passed in silence. Fred was hearing the hardest thing to accept that he'd ever heard in his entire life. Here, within his arms he held the most beautiful, loving woman he'd ever dreamed of having; and she was telling him that, while she surely and truly loved him, he could never possess her. She was clever, all right. She was laying down her terms for their relationship.

"I suppose I'll have to make do when it pleases you, then? We'll be an 'item,' then. Is that how you'd like it?" Fred winced a bit as if he was about to have his arm severed. He began reconciling himself to those times when he could have her and love her; and he began accepting that. Naturally, it wasn't logical to expect a notorious porn star to dote on him alone. He reflected longer:

'I'll have to be content to watch her films when she's away from me. I'll have to slake my lust for her by imagining she is in my arms when she is in some other man's arms. I'll hold her close in my dreams and dream of those times when I have possessed her; and I'll obsess over licking her delicious vagina and kissing her signature butterfly tattooed upper thighs. But I WILL have her sometimes; and that will have to be enough. There's no changing her; no use even thinking I could ever do that.

'Maybe I'll love her more, because she IS a whore; and a totally opposite kind of woman from Petunia. Maybe I love her because I know she loves making love with me. She gets great pleasure from our love making and I love to see her enjoying her pleasure. I know I'll never get enough of her. I just love being with her. I guess that's what love is. I don't understand why I love her; but I know I do love her. Yes, I definitely do love her. I'll accept her terms. There's no use trying to fight her. If I did that, I wouldn't have her at all; and I know it.'

He shrugged his shoulders, las if lifting his questions higher into the air. Marty hadn't answered his questions and she wasn't about to. She only let her eyes smile her little girl smile, knowing that Fred would agree to have the relationship on her terms. Her demand was final.

"Okay, you win," he cocked his head and lifted his opened hands. He was a solitary sort of man anyway, he told himself.

"Besides," Marty sat on his lap and kissed him as if to reassure him she really wasn't going anywhere, *"you are still married, Fred.*

Wouldn't you honestly rather be part time with a naughty, wanton sex object like me than full time with an easily managed, steady woman like your wife? I'd be very hard to tame, Fred. I could never be a domestic sort of woman.

"*You'd constantly be chasing after me and hunting me down. You might even need to drag me out of other men's beds or off the stages where I was performing live porn. I believe you'd get exhausted from all the tracking and chasing. It would be hard to catch and possess me. Do you honestly think that would be fun for you? Do you think you'd like to put yourself through all those challenges just to be my main man, my truest lover? Wouldn't you rather if I signaled to you when I need you to catch me?*" Marty smiled her most coquettish smile, inviting Fred to chase her.

"*I can handle any challenge. I've never met a challenge I couldn't handle.*" grinned a confident Fred. "*I want you, Marty. I want your eyes to look at, your lips to kiss, and your body for how you make me feel. I want to have that hot connection my body feels whenever you touch me. You've made me feel like a man again for the first time in years.*"

"Oh, Fred, you wonderful darling," she whispered in a sincere seductive tone, "*You're surprising me, sweetheart! That's such a delicious thought!*" Her breast swelled. She felt victorious joy for herself and a tinge of pity for Fred's addiction to her at the same time.

"*Fred, sweetheart, do you believe you could still feel this way about me after we've made love in some new positions? I'd like to first experiment doing all sorts of sexy things with you. Let's find out if you'll enjoy playing sex games with me and chasing me. You haven't even tied me to your bed posts and made me your love slave, yet.*

"*Wouldn't you like to know how you feel while you keep my legs propped open and apart and I can't close them, while you slap your hands on my ass? I want you to really dominate me the next time we play. I want you to use my nipple clamps, a blindfold, and my leg spreader. I'd like you to tease me with my vibrator and some feathers, too. I want you to drive me crazy to have your wonderful penis inside me. I love being stimulated out of my mind while I'm making love. Would you like to do those things with me, Fred? I'd like you to strip away my pretense of virtue and make love with me while I'm so stimulated that I have to beg you to stop. I'd love feeling dominated and ravaged like that. I want you to make me feel like I'm your obedient bitch. I want those feelings of need to please you sweeping through my blood and getting me hotter than fire, Fred.*

"You'll play those sexy BDSM games with me, won't you, darling? You'll chase me around the villa and you'll play with me and make love with me in all the different rooms, won't you? Please say yes to me. You know how much I love having fun. I want to experience every feeling imaginable while you are ravaging me with your wonderful penis." she purred while stroking his cock.

"Yes, yes, a thousand times yes. We'll play all sorts of sex games, Babe; whatever pleases you. I'm up for it!" Fred smiled his *'you win'* smile. His home would become Marty's playpen.

"Wonderful! We have so many new and exciting things we need to explore, sweetheart. I'd feel dreadfully awful if you ever thought I was dull and boring! What we have right now is special. We can build so much on that. It will be wonderful, I promise you. Let's play some naughty sex games together a few times. Let's pretend you are deflowering me, taking away my chastity; and then we'll talk more about whether being serious would be better than having fun, okay?" her soft temptress voice cooed in his ear while she stroked his cock and nibble kissed his cheek.

Like an elusive trophy animal, Marty knew she needed to stay a step ahead of her pursuer. She put on her coat and left for her place, knowing her teasing would play upon Fred's mind and drive him crazy. He'd lust for her even more. He'd imagine he still had a chance of possessing her. She'd keep reeling him in, but she'd stop short of going to the marriage altar.

Marty intended to tighten her line on Fred. She didn't want marriage. But she did want money. Separating her man from his money without yielding to the temptation of marriage is every top courtesan's most highly prized art. Marty knew her talents were up to the task. She calculated how she'd manage their time. They'd enjoy coitus all evening Friday, and all-day Saturday; she'd let him tie her up and pretend he was her master and she, his slave; and she'd moan and beg for more sex. After they played, she'd suggest they go to a secluded country restaurant in a nearby town. She believed he was now completely comfortable being seen with her.

She'd spend Saturday evening with him. She'd get out of bed first on Sunday morning and make herself fresh as a morning daisy. She'd have a mint tasting mouth. She'd wear alluring make up with sexy taupe eye shadow. And her vagina would be gardenia scented and yummy delicious to taste. Her vagina would invite Fred with its creamiest, freshest, tastiest best offering ever. She'd return to bed and wake him with probing soul kisses. They'd perform oral sex all morning until they were both famished. She'd convince him that the happiness of his cock had become her life's only priority.

After a late breakfast at another upscale restaurant, she'd tell him she'd love to stay overnight with him much more often, but she'd need another twenty million for the Firm's management to justify her time; unless, of course, he wanted to pay her three hundred thousand dollars from his checking account. He'd pay her, of that she felt certain; but she hoped to learn something by how she got paid.

Whichever account the money came from, investment transfer, checking, or cash she'd know Petunia didn't have access to see it. When he next pushed the marriage idea and got serious about it, she'd tell him that he'd need to first prove he really loved only her by giving her power of attorney controls over all the investment accounts that Petunia could still access. As the family's financial advisor, she would need to be placed in charge of Petunia's disbursements. She'd become Petunia's money manager. With Fred's silent approval she'd systematically drain Petunia's finances and poison the formalities that remained of their marriage. She'd turn spouse against spouse; while always being sexually available for Fred. Until she gained that financial power, she'd thank Fred for memorable weeks and weekends and continue their romantic rendezvous.'

After seeing Fred often over several more weeks, Marty suggested a bold, masterful stroke, designed to appeal to his ego. They lay side by side in bed one evening when she broached her daring scheme.

MANIPIPULATE

"Fred, darling," she' cooed, stroking his cock after coitus, *"Let's teach that wife of yours that it's just not fair for her to go gallivanting off and leaving you all by your lonesome self the way she does. Let's show your friends that you're not going to stand for her neglect anymore. Let's go to one of those gala wild game parties that your hunting club throws.*

"I'll dress to the nines in a stunning black low-cut dress that drops far below my naval, all the way down to the very top of my vagina; and I'll wear a shining red ruby in my naval. I'll wear a diamond choker with another ruby, my largest. It hangs on a chain of diamonds and plunges all the way down into my cleavage. The dress I'll wear will be a transparent gown of gauze-like material that has open slits on the sides to accent my legs. It's made of a sinfully soft, clinging silky-mesh material. I look yummy delicious in it. I'll wear

it without a bra, of course. It partially exposes my breasts. You'll love seeing me in it. I promise you; your mouth will water. Let's have some fun, Fred." She ran her finger down his forehead and nose, and then touched his lips. Then she kissed him. She knew he couldn't refuse her.

"You want us to have our own private coming out party, don't you, Babe," smiled Fred. The idea of making a splash in front of his friends appealed to him.

"Oh, yes, my darling, I do, I really do!" She squealed with delight and adroitly changed her position to lap dance; and then deftly slid Fred's penis into her hot slippery vagina. *"I desperately want to free myself from my cocoon and spread my wings, Fred. I want to feel as free as a butterfly to flutter and make love; and I want everyone to see me walk into that ball room with you.*

"When your friends see me on your arm, they'll know you have a real live trophy; the finest in the world. They'll all envy you. I want everyone to look up to you, darling. Every man in that ball room will wish he was you. I can do that for you. And I want to. You'll see. Every man will respect you as their top alpha male. When they see me in that provocative dress, they'll all immediately understand that you are having your manly ways with me. And if anyone dares to suggest that you're paying me, I'll just squeeze myself up tightly against you and kiss your cheek, and I'll beam my star-struck peepers at him, and I'll tell him that you've never had to pay me for anything." She steadily, rhythmically made love with Fred while selling her plan. She felt his cock swelling inside her.

"We'll make a spectacularly grand entrance," she continued while slowing the pace of her thrusts on his cock. *"You can introduce me as your personal love slave, like you own me, sweetheart. That will make every man jealous of you. I'll wear black mascara and long thick eyelashes. I'll wear my extra-long black nails; and*

I'll paint lines on my face that flare out like a pussy cat's whiskers." She bared her teeth and fanned her fingers away from her face, pretending they were cat whiskers.

"I'll look sexier than every other woman there, I promise you, darling. You'll be the talk of your club! Would you like that?"

"Why yes, my love, you've gotten me in the mood," Fred's eyes twinkled. His mind reveled in its image of conqueror. Marty's psychological manipulation was working to perfection. All men had egos. Hunters' egos were bigger than most; and Fred's ego towered above all of them. She recognized the egomania in Fred's eyes. It was her cue to capture and harness it to her advantage.

"To make the perfect impression, I should wrap my see-through pussy cat dress in a white mink stole," she purred. *"The evenings are much cooler now, Fred; and I don't want my precious warm vagina to feel chilled. I'd purchase one myself, but I wouldn't want to dress in something that you might not like, darling."*

She knew Fred would act on her suggestion. How could he resist teaching his wife a lesson, being the envy of his friends and goading them about his sexual prowess all at the same time? For another twenty million under the Firm's management Marty would make it all possible for him. Her commission payment would be three hundred thousand dollars. The firm would pay her, making her representation to Fred's friends the truth.

And, likely at the gala gathering, she'd discover other wealthy men might also wish to know her better. But she never mentioned that coincidental thought to Fred. She didn't fully explain all the features of her dress either.

On the night of Marty's grand social entrance, she arrived in a fully sleeved, floor length white lynx fur coat, loosely draped over her transparent pussy cat ensemble, complements of her benefactor and lover. Fred insisted that she be adorned in the most luxurious garment the most exclusive local furrier had to offer. A mere mink stole simply wouldn't do. Any hunter could provide a woman with one of those, but only Fred could immerse his prized trophy whore in a floor length lynx. *"No gift is too great for you, Marty. Everything pales in comparison to beautiful adorable you and your magnificent, glorious, penis pleasing, vagina,"* he beamed proudly while presenting the fur; and then hugged her with sincere heartfelt love while he kissed her full on her mouth.

CHAPTER TWO

The silliest woman can manage a clever man: but it takes a very clever woman to manage a fool: Rudyard Kipling: Three and an Extra)

Like the sweet apple which reddens upon the topmost bough, atop the topmost twig- which the pluckers forgot somehow- forgot it not, nay, for none could get it 'til now (Dante Gabriel Rossetti: Beauty; A combination from Sappha)

An ordinary man cheats on his spouse; an emboldened man consorts with a whore; but only an exceptionally strong-willed man has the courage to bind his soul to the soul of a thoroughly immoral whore: Rosemary Ness-Bitner, author)

EXHIBIT

Marty's grand entrance was a spectacular success. The ballroom was the largest indoor meeting facility in Plaintown, spanning the length and width of a football field. As Marty entered the cavernous ballroom's illuminated foyer, hundreds of sex thirsting male eyes stared hungrily. A living oasis was about to descend into their midst. She opened her coat widely, allowing every feasting eye to appreciate her unbounded sexuality. Her black gauze garment created a misty see-through effect, revealing her glistening, creamy white skin underneath. When she moved in her dress, the softness of its material naturally stimulated her nipples and vagina, arousing her. Its back had a plunge line that descended noticeably below her waist, touching the top crevasse of her muscle toned derriere. She walked slowly to the top stair, paused, and stood there.

'Let them stare. You're drawing in all their eyes now. Wait until you feel their hunger for you; then descend the stairs.' Miss Promiscuity was always right about seductions.

When Marty walked, her dress accented the outline of her derriere. Men's eyes salivated. They readily imagined Marty's highly toned behind twerking their penises. The see-through material worked its temptation magic. It hugged her hips and clung tightly against her frontal concavity. Like a magnet, the dress captured eyeballs' gazes, carried them naturally downward to discover her honey spot; then held them there, fixated in wonder. It riveted them in place.

Refusing to be distracted, men stared. Their eyes first took in Marty and her outrageously near naked body sheer; but then, unable to resist where her dress took their eyes, they laser focused their gazes on her definer of womanhood. They all wanted what they saw. Her presentation was an unmistakably bold pronouncement. Her beautiful nipples visibly protruded into the smoke-colored, tissue-gauze dress, proudly boasting their unmistakable cherry red offerings. The dress fearlessly invited hungry lips to suckle her nipples. It was a very clever dress, first coaxing all eyes to gaze upon the provocative allure of Marty's cherry bud nipples; then, also convincing the spellbound that it struggled mightily to contain them; shield them from ravaging male hands and lips; all the while knowing with certainty that this was destined to be an epic struggle that the flimsy dress would surely lose, later, in some secluded, intimate place.

Meanwhile, the provocateur dress lead searching eyes lower, as if holding their visions by their hands; pulling them downward, ever lower and still lower, until they finally rested upon the mysterious tempting delight which the salacious garment artfully, suggestively, intended to reveal all along. The dress could not be fooled. It understood what males' eyes desired. It knew its seduction role. And it played it perfectly. It teased those lust starved eyes; invited their eager hands to touch the woman it so poorly shielded. And it begged them to tear it open; rip it away from her; discard it; seize and ravage the delicious prize that was barely restrained inside it.

And the eyes noticed. Brazenly visible below the sheer dress's low plunge line; behind its clinging transparency, clearly beckoned Marty's deliciously revealed, mysterious love channel. The thin, mist-like film of the dress, by design, artfully tried but abjectly failed to conceal Marty's infamous treasure. It showcased her inviting sexuality beautifully. It proclaimed that her shameless immorality had no rival. It was artfully designed to highlight her beckoning, shadowy sweet spot; delivered and served up upon carefree butterfly wings.

Eyes looked closer at this marvel in their midst; noting that her luscious love channel was flanked by alluring mounds of glistening, creamy white flesh. And, temptingly revealed upon her upper thighs, faintly visible beneath the transparent smoke gauze, appeared her bright yellow-orange Monarch Butterfly tattoo. It brazenly mocked social norms, proclaiming it offered its availability to those who sought freedom's liberation. It invited male gazers to come closer to it; enter it and explore its uninhibited wonders. It messaged, not subtly; but boldly, that it was available and eager to spread its engulfing wings over their cocks; welcoming their capitulations to lust.

Everything else in the ballroom: the people, the exhibits, Fred, her coat, the rest of her voluptuous body and gorgeous face, were all merely side shows and accessories to Marty's breathtakingly ravenous, whoring, unashamed vagina. She stood confidently at the top of the ballroom's stairs and opened wide her white full-length lynx, presenting her yearning accommodative pleasure tempting center behind its transparent gauze wrapper. She turned her head slowly back and forth and smiled her most winsome smile.

She made her silent announcement that informed the men on the floor below:

'Here before you, is a different sort of woman; the kind you often secretly want. You don't need to seek me in secret any longer. I am here and now. Come to me.'

Marty played her entrance to the hilt. She took in a deep breath while arching her back, accentuating her exceptional breasts. Her fingers found the ruby that dangled at the top of her cleavage. She slowly, innocently, and suggestively, raised it up and down over her breasts, while invitingly licking her lower lip.

She closed her eyes, dreamily as if she was being stimulated by compliant fingers; and smiled again. Then, she reached her hand down to the top of her vagina and slowly gyrated her hips in a subtle, barely noticeable, forward, and back rocking motion, as if she was initiating copulations with an imaginary penis. She took a deep breath while opening her mouth and extending her tongue. She was intentionally attracting more attention than a billboard. She was in no hurry to leave her coming out platform.

She waited while hundreds of men stopped conversing to look up and notice her; then bask their approving, nodding heads in the radiant allure of her wanton vagina. Some of them visibly salivated at the sight of her feminine wares. She noticed. Then, smiling broadly at all of them, she allowed Fred to remove her coat and take it away for safekeeping. Sin, sex, and lust, packaged brilliantly in mouth-watering appeal, had arrived.

Her dress performed perfectly. It appeared to struggle in a hopeless, losing battle; trying futilely to contain Marty's delightful breasts. Her up-lilted nipples showed plainly through the stretched fabric, inviting all who saw them to fondle them; kiss them; nibble them; pinch them; lick them; adore them. The garment's flimsy gauze clung so tightly to the concavity of Marty's upper thighs; it gave the appearance that its threads might split apart at any second from anyone's innocent touching. Clearly visible behind its gossamer veil, Marty's rapacious vagina presented its mystique and allure. It was the delicious punctuation mark to Marty's unmistakably ribald, declaration of her commitment to shameless immorality. Behind the flimsy mesh her butterfly tattoo and its nubile honey pot chafed to be freed from the troublesome garment. Her body seemed to plead with the men below her:

'Come free me, like the butterfly I represent,' the mouthwatering idol of fecundity begged her audience. *'Kiss my honey pot; stimulate me with your tongues and fingers; enter me with your penises; and hurry!'* The men gathered below appreciated the butterfly's message. They imagined their hands might be the fortunate feeler feet of a mating Monarch, clawing away the annoying gauze dress, freeing this bodacious butterfly sex goddess from her sterile cocoon. They dared to hope it would soon break free and flutter to them, to rest upon their faces and penises. And, it would! Tonight, would be historic for this hunters' club. Marty's guiltless vagina chafed to free itself; to flutter above every constraint and inhibition; and make club history happen.

Her mind was already free. She visualized her vagina fluttering above the hundred erect cocks below her, visiting each of them in their turn. She fantasized hovering above each man's individual cock, engulfing it securely in her hot slippery vagina until it ejaculated its semen into her. She wondered how many of their cocks with their pasty cum offerings she'd eventually conquer. How many among them would discover her unquenchably wanton vagina? She savored a lustful thought:

'I have entered a whore's paradise!' How many essential expressions of male love, their semen's' creams, their irrefutable proof of

surrender, their sweetness love will become mine, all mine? Tonight, I will, most certainly, leave my cocoon. After this night I will no longer be secreted in social obscurity. I will be fluttering freely, highly visible, dazzlingly beautiful; noticed by all. From this night forward, my reputation as a shameless guiltless whore and porn goddess will precede me.

'Many of these men will ask about me. Many will buy my porn films. They will see how sensual I am while I perform my seductions and my threesomes. They will salivate while they watch me while I lovingly lick penises and perform fellatio; and they will become passion crazed when they see me fornicate, bouncing on cocks, and twerking cocks, and fucking cock in my maiden position; performing in so many different scenes and positions. They will appreciate my immorality when the notice I often wear my black skirts and red tops, promoting my love of anarchy. They will gasp at how I revel in my fornications and become spellbound, seeing how I rejoice while I orgasm. They will imagine that it is they who are holding me onto their penises while I orgasm. They will become crazed while they watch my partners' semen streams spilling onto my eager tongue and from my penis-loving vagina; and they will pine for the day when that fornication experience with me and those semen streams from my vagina will be theirs. Tonight, I will become notorious. I will become labeled; and known as the most immoral, incorrigible, marriage-wrecking whore in Plaintown. As these boys would say: Tonight, I will put my best game on the field. In their minds, I will create my most unforgettable, must-have-me film. I will leave every-thing I've got on the field. And every man here will love and want me.'

Heads looked up, seeing at once an uninhibited woman seductress who shamelessly offered them a cornucopia of sensa-tional sex, unimaginable sinful pleasures, and a bubbly, fun loving eagerness to give their lusts full satisfaction. The boldness of her winsome smile, passion craving, pussy cat alluring eyes, and irresistible curvaceous body signaled her unmistakable invitation to every man below:

'Come visit me. I want us to play together. Would you like to pleasure me? I know you would. Don't be shy. I'm not. I shamelessly sleep around. I'm the girl who says 'yes' to all your sinful requests. I will gleefully fuck and suck you. We'll have fun! Call me!'

She twisted her body slightly, as if to learn Fred's progress with checking her coat, while giving her assembled hopefuls a clear view of her delicious profile.

Many faces flushed red when they first saw her. Conversations were toppled mid-sentence like hapless innocent trees felled by hurricane force winds. Jaws of a hundred onlookers gaped open. They witnessed a miracle sex goddess making an unscheduled visit to mankind. An eerie silence fell upon these men. A mysterious invisible eraser passed across their minds, creating collective amnesia. No longer did they concern themselves about which rifle or hunt they might acquire. No longer did they give thought or consideration to the women who accompanied them to the ball. These men experienced a collective mesmerizing passion-lust. Every one of them desired the beautiful woman at the top of the stairs.

Instantly, each individual mind was transported to its private imaginary dream world. There it basked in lovely scents, soft pillows, and amorous music. In their dream worlds the men kissed her, made love with her, performed cunnilingus with her; and assumed every position and used every intimacy toy imaginable to excite her feelings and please her. They imagined she smiled approvingly while they did these amorous things. All wished for her boundless happiness from their love making.

Every man's imagination briefly imagined his cock partaking of her favors; many also visualized their face cupped firmly to her sex, and their tongues pleasuring her. Every man imagined he could forsake all others; somehow wish away and release himself from all his familial responsibilities, hold this gorgeous sin-loving creature closely in his arms; and make love with her, forever.

Slowly, this collective swoon dispelled to reality as whispers and murmurs returned to refill the silence. But, unspoken torrents of insatiable lust raged and surged in the undertow of these observers' arteries. These barely controlled torrents threatened to burst unchecked, like swollen flash floods, onto thirsting desert floors. There was an undercurrent of eagerness that sought to facilitate every scintilla of unbridled whoring the alluring, delicious nymph might desire. Many secret pledges were made to accommodate every sinful promiscuous wish she might request of their lust-parched souls, if only she would offer them the chance.

The primal limbic urge to quench their sudden passion thirsts swept away all these men's other thoughts. They were awestruck in a similar way as the prehistoric cave dwellers that marveled at the animal herds on Lascaux's ceilings, or in the same reverent humility one feels when looking up at the magnificence that adorns the Sistine Chapel's ceiling. They instinctively knew a deity, albeit a sin-obsessed one, graced their presence. By their hushed silence Marty knew she had achieved her desired effect.

She knew and understood men. She knew many cocks were suddenly feeling an unmistakable throbbing sensation. She knew hot, fresh blood was rushing unchecked, into many of these hopeful penises, causing them to proudly rise; stand strong and stiff and willing to perform for her. They hoped to make their intimate acquaintances with her. Many of these men would declare their interest and come forth this very evening. They would offer whatever she wished for her pleasure. An overwhelming communal urge swept the ball room. Trousers bulged; cocks were at the ready. Marty's sense of men was unerring. Many would approach her.

Miss promiscuity's voice whispered again to Marty:

'This is your moment. Descend those stairs by yourself, while Fred checks your coat. Proudly telegraph to everyone that no one man owns you. Smile at all of them, make many eye contacts, lift your eyebrows, smile, and wet your lips as you take each step. Signal to them that you are available. Let your face beam to every eye.

'Invite their approaches. Express your desire to help their cocks explore your slippery hot vagina by the sensuous motion of your hips. Show them how you yearn to have their cocks discover your mouth by your lips' playful purses between your sinful smiles. Help them realize you want them to hold and kiss you; you want them to fondle your breasts and tongue-tease your buds.

'Help their imaginations know you want them to kiss you on your ruby-studded stomach and below; down to the lowest cut of your dress, and lower still, to your wonder place. Let them know they are welcome to slake their love thirsting tongues inside your lust fountain. Help them understand you burn with desire. Assure them that you yearn to suck and fuck them in unimaginable, lust pleasuring ways; that they'll always remember. Be your confident, fun loving, promiscuous whoring best.'

Marty's calculation to wear her revealing tissue-dress with its provocative leg slits would prove prescient. These were all aggressive alpha males with keen eyes for world class big game trophies, magnificent horseflesh, superior automobiles and airplanes, and the legs of beautiful women. The dress's leg slit revealed sculptured, enticing continuous firmness from her foot all the way up to her waist. Imagination stimulation worked its magic. Audible gasps sounded in the ballroom below. Ladylike deportment was not the impression Marty sought to make.

Her dress and mannerisms were intended to pique males' interest from complacency; make them desire more; stimulate their imaginations to think what might be possible; and, stimulate a marketing buzz that would last long after this night. Her scheme worked brilliantly. No debutant ever aroused male excitement on her 'coming out ball' that approached the enthusiasm Marty generated with her 'putting out' proclamation night. Her sensual dramaturgy sparkled. She outshined the most dazzling scene and repertoire of every actress of stage and film.

Men looking up from the ballroom floor saw a sex goddess partially revealed, a nubile nymph deity in a transparent smoke-gauze dress. The implication of the dress was unmistakable. The woman wrapped inside it was a beautiful human butterfly, seeking to emerge from its cocoon; seeking to freely flutter and cavort in the glory of nature.

Soon, with some lucky someone, surely the symbolic dress would fall away, freeing the female muse from its ridiculous attempt at concealment, revealing this sumptuous woman's beautiful nakedness. Some lucky man among them would likely savor that darker channel between her legs with his lips and penetrate it with his penis; perhaps before this night would end.

Women looking up from the ballroom floor had an entirely different vision. That dress and the woman within it threatened them. The garment appeared cleaved into halves by the ominous darkened channel threat that lurked within the concavity of Marty's hips. That channel was the loathsome dread to women who held some form of control power over their husbands; and it struck terror in the minds of those women whose status and life styles existed at the pleasures of their husbands.

They had often suffered silently while their husband and friends made snide remarks and jokes about women. They resented their situations but tolerated them for the creature comforts their men provided them. These women knew they were completely vulnerable to the whore.

The alarming message all women received starkly contrasted with the beckoning message which the godless pathway invitation was broadcasting to their men. The women noticed Marty flaunting her vagina; implying how it desperately strained and chafed to burst free of its tissue wrapping dress. They knew it boldly proclaimed it wanted to open for business and pleasure. Clearly, it welcomed exploration by the hands, cocks, and tongues of their men. They intuited, correctly, that it didn't care one iota about their civilities, or social niceties; or about how it would surely plunge some of their lives into turmoil. It was there; just there; and boldly proclaiming it was mindless of social niceties and unconcerned with their feelings.

It stood there, above all of them, as if on a pedestal, proclaiming that it would pay no attention to their pretentious boundaries. It would fuck whomever it pleased. By her obvious, prolonged flaunting at the top of the stairs, Marty alerted these women that she would be a determined adversary. Beckoning their men to come hither, while noticing these wives of her insouciance about their acceptance or approval, was the genius of her dress selection. No other garment could have delivered her intentions better.

An icy chill shot through the women's veins. Instinctively, they understood Marty's foreboding channel was an immediate danger to their settled lives. Subliminally, they understood that it yearned to slice through its paper-thin garment. It further sought to sever Plaintown's society women from their marital moorings and intended to slash and render the social fabric that secured their ordered world.

It threatened them like an ominous heartless dagger, poised to pierce their hearts; handily performing the will of its director, the conniving mind of this intrusive brazen whore. They sensed that the interloper had instantly fueled their men's minds with desires and ignited their blood with lust-fires. This awareness shock sent chills through their blood. Fear struck then as, one by one, they looked up and saw what their men had already assessed. There, posing flagrantly and unashamedly atop the ballroom's stairs stood their worst nightmare. Marty read the room, taking everything in. Her confident smiles beamed promiscuity's promise to the men, and mockery to the women. She already knew, from her WEX years, what to expect from these people. She would be fawned over and adored by the men; snubbed and rejected by the women.

Before this night the society mavens of Plaintown had only a dim awareness of this predator femme fatale. Some had heard of the goings on at Sustacks, but it seemed far away from them and irrelevant. After all, Sustack's was a Jewish firm and they kept their business strictly with white Anglo Saxon Protestant firms. But after seeing Marty's pussy cat display dress, the female talk circuit blazed with reaction. Respectable, highly socialized women, who never gave one conscience moment's concern over their husbands' murders of innocent animals, suddenly sounded alarms that their cushy life styles might fall victim to this seductive huntress, now challenging their womanhood in their very midst.

CHAPTER THREE

The time and my intents are savage wild, more fierce, and more inexorable by far than empty tigers or the roaring sea (William Shakespeare: Romeo and Juliet)

Loving without understanding why; while never loving enough, became her passion. Her quest eluded her; and her loves all loved her (Rosemary Ness- Bitner: author)

WHAT?

First female gossip, incredulous:

"What was Fred thinking? What in hell did he think would happen; bringing a slut like that, a porn star, no less, a completely immoral woman who makes money by fucking her ass off, to a party with two hundred alpha male big game hunters? And what was she thinking? That she'd make every man into one of her prostitution clients? I'll bet that's exactly what she thought, the shameless bitch! And where did she acquire that smoky gauze dress? Was it imported from France? I bet it was. They wear skimpy flimsy things like that over there. Did you see how her red nipple buttons protruded? They stuck right out there. No bra.

"And did you see how clearly her vagina channel showed? She was really advertising; putting it right out there for any man who wanted it. She had to know her dress was that transparent. I could see right through it. She might as well have been naked! Where did she find those diamond studded heels? They don't sell those around

here. Did you notice how that butterfly tattoo on her thighs matched the butterfly pin in her hair? Was that some subtle signal that she works her vagina and her mouth simultaneously? Do you think that pin was studded with real rubies? I thought they were real. I'll bet Fred bought that for her. And her full-length Lynx, too! Did you get a look at that huge ruby that graced her boobs? Yes, I know Fred isn't cheap. But what is she? Is she Fred's new woman or is she everyman's whore; or both? I hope she stays happy with Fred. She better stay away from my Bert."

Marty had broken into the tightly guarded inner circle of the hypocrite herd!

Second female gossip, alarmed:

"How did this happen? Who let her in? Was it Fred? Really? Where did he find her, or did she find him? We have a serious problem. Phyllis told me that her friend did some research. She said that Marty woman makes dirty porno movies. Yes! She even made a film having an orgy with eight black men! Yes! They took turns fucking her in every orifice for two whole hours. Yes, blacks! Phyliss said that didn't make any difference to her. She's probably color blind.

"HELL YES, Phyliss said she enjoyed it. Yes, every minute of it! Their lips nibbled her nipples and their hands felt her everywhere, all over her body. When they weren't fucking her, they had their fingers in her. She was being stimulated the entire time. Phyliss said she couldn't imagine how a woman could enjoy sex that much for that long. No, she wasn't the least bit afraid! Phyliss said she loved it!

"They even had oral sex with her. Yes, I'm telling you. What do you think I mean? They licked her vagina. No, several of them did that. Phyllis said she encouraged them to do that. She planted her sex right on top of their faces, like she begged them to lick her. Her face beamed! She oohed and ahhhed the whole time. She loved it.

Phyllis said so. Yes, she sucked them too, licked their balls while her fingers stroked their cocks. Yes, she did it all. She even sucked some of them while some others were licking her.

"I can't imagine how any woman could concentrate like that. She even stroked them until they came right inside her mouth. Phyllis said she never saw a woman more wanton and uninhibited in her life. She begged her partners to fuck her more and harder through the entire movie. Phyllis said she's sure she watched her have at least seven orgasms. No, not Phyllis, Marty, Marty had the seven orgasms. She was screaming how much she loved it, telling them to give her all they had, all through the movie:

'Oh, my God, that's a lot of cocks! I love it, love it! Wheee! Ohhh! Yes, yes, yes! It feels soooo goood to be getting fucked by so many cocks! Wheee, Ohhh, Yes, yes, I'm going to come. Ohhh, I'm coming again! Oh, that feels sooo gooood! Yes, fuck me more, fuck me more. Who's next? Who will please fuck my vagina next?'

"Phyllis said the whole film was unreal. She said it put her mind into another world. She said she'd never imagined any woman could possibly be that fuck-crazed. She said she had to pinch herself to make sure she wasn't just imagining the whole thing; and then she watched it a second time. She said that, in its sinful, disgusting way, it was beautiful; but there was no plot to it.

"You can't blame the men for wanting her. No, you really can't. She has a fabulous body, but it's her face that captivates them. It's so perfect, so beautiful. It's child-like and inviting when she smiles. She makes the man feel like it's his God-ordered obligation to surrender to her, like she's a farmer's sweet innocent daughter; and she's asking him to meet her in the hayloft and fuck her; and like there's something internally wrong with him if he doesn't at least try; or like he'll be a failure of a man if he doesn't offer himself to her. She comes off like she's a goddess or something. She stood at the top of those stairs for the longest time, posturing proudly.

She acted like she expected us to worship her, instead of God. She has no concept of modesty. She acts like it's perfectly natural for a man to forget his morals and put his hands all over her. She makes the man feel like that's the right and reasonable thing for him to do; like she expects it of him. She encourages it, by acting like her immoral behavior is perfectly normal.

"Oh, she knows what she's got going all right. She loves it when men throw themselves at her. Mary Lou says she's a shameless nymphomaniac. Yes, she is unstoppable! Sex is a joy for her. Well, Mary Lou says she lives for it. She can't ever get enough of it! I don't know if it was a good film or not, as those trashy things go. That's not my point, Dorothy! Good heavens, Dorothy. Will you wake up? I'm not going to get it to watch it with Bert. Do you think I'm crazy? You're not in Kansas anymore, you know. This barbarian, this whore, has crashed our gates!"

Third female gossip, confirming the second female gossip:

"Evelyn was positively shocked, Millie. A tightening circle of about fifty men surrounded her. She drew more interest than any of the gun displays or guided hunt exhibits. She didn't even pay for a booth. She decided where she was going to show herself off. Yes, it was right in the middle of the ballroom floor. The men were all around her, like a pack of hounds jostling for position. They were spilling their liquor on themselves; and sniffing after her, like she was a bitch dog in heat; and they acted like dogs, yelping and howling at her antics.

"It started impromptu. Evelyn was only standing a few feet away. Burnett, Johnson, and Windham were close to her, asking her questions like who she came with, and how did she like big game hunting. You know, they were just making small talk, when she says:

'Oh, Fred's off looking at some guns somewhere. He just left me here, all by lonesome. I feel so abandoned. A girl likes to be paid attention to; don't you know? A girl likes to be hugged and kissed; and touched all over; and made to feel like she's beautiful, and loved and appreciated. She likes to feel sexy and wanted by a man, don't you boys know that?'

"*She knew exactly what she was doing. Her display at the top of the ballroom stairs had kindled the sparks of limbic lust in every man in the ballroom. Now she decided to pour gasoline on those lusts. She wanted every man there to know that she was deliciously, shamelessly profligate; that she was a fallen woman who had no desire to be rescued; that she was flagrantly, wantonly immoral; and that she loved herself for being the opposite of every descent woman there. Burnett and Windham intuited what she wanted to accomplish that night. They looked at each other and smiled, signaling that they were willing to play along with her game.*

"*That's when Jim Windham got things going. He slid around behind her and put his arms around her stomach. She giggled and yelped and oohed and aahed, signaling that was what she wanted; and encouraging him to do more of what he was doing. Then, she shoved her backside right into him, real deliberately; obviously like; and hard. She ground her ass into Jim's groin while he stood behind her; twisting and bumping her ass against Jim's pecker, like she wanted it inside her. She was asking for it!*

"*That signaled Johnson and Burnett to keep going. Jim told her to fall back into him and lay her head on his shoulder. When she did that, he started kissing her neck. She giggled, real casual and natural, like she loved what he was doing and like she had no concerns about what the rest of us thought of her. Then she dispelled all doubts about the sort of woman she is.*

"*Yes, Millie, right there on the ballroom floor. She reached behind her and started stroking Jim's cock. No, she wasn't embarrassed; not in the slightest. She did that right out in the open where everyone could see her, squeezing Jim's cock, right through his pants. No, she didn't hesitate at all. She went right for it, like she did it all the time. She wanted to play. Yes, Millie; of course, with his cock. Well, what else would you expect from a porn star?*

"No, Jim didn't pull away. He loved what she was doing. In truth, I think he was falling in love with her. Yes, she has that effect on men. Then, Burnett and Johnson hugged her and began kissing her cheeks. Well, she just turned her head to their faces and started kissing them both, right on their lips; real slut-like. Yes, even while she was stroking Jim's cock. She was in her element, I'm telling you. She was dousing every male's limbic fire with gasoline. I swear, Millie, every man in that ballroom got a hard-on, just watching her. She was giving Burnett and Johnson those long, soulful, tongue in their mouths kind of kisses; you know, like you'd expect a pagan, godless porn star whore to do. And then she asked:

'Will you gentlemen mind terribly if a girl feels like being naughty?'

"At first the crowd members eyed one another nervously, as if they shouldn't be standing there watching something forbidden. But then one man howled like a coon hound on a scent. Everyone gasped at what she did next. The crowd grew larger. Nobody wanted to miss her goings-on. You wouldn't believe what that shameless whore did next. She took Burnett's and Johnson's hands and lifted them up; guided them right inside her flimsy dress and positioned them right smack upon her breasts. Then she giggled and teased them:

'Won't you boys feel my breasts and pinch my nipples? I love it when a man does that. It gets my vagina all hot and excited. I want to be in the mood tonight.'

"She intentionally egged them on, Millie. She wanted them feeling her and groping her. She liked it. Yes, she was totally shameless. She behaved like everything she did was natural and reasonable. There was not one single sign of a moral twinge or hint of hesitation or uncertainty about her willfulness. It was like she was performing

her warm up act on a porn set, right there; live before our very eyes. Well, Burnett and Johnson pinched her nipples and fondled her; and with their free hands they reached through the slits in her dress and squeezed her ass while she was stroking their dicks and kissing both of them. Her face beamed a rosy red and she giggled, saying:

'Now I'm finally feeling like you men appreciate me. A woman loves being touched; don't you know? Ohhh, yes; I love that. That feels really, good.'

"I'm telling you Millie; she wasn't just saying that. She really did love it. Millie, I kid you not. Men's eyes were popping out of their sockets. They were whooping and spilling their drinks watching her; seeing how she enjoyed having her tits fondled and her ass being squeezed like that. The crowd around her deepened to eight or ten men thick. Even the booth tenders left their posts unguarded, with their guns and accessories just lying there. They wanted to gawk at her goings on. I never saw anything like it before! Never in my life!

"And, she just kept it up and kept it up. She had no intention of stopping. I was starting to wonder if this would end up with her fucking some men right there on the floor. She obviously wanted to be seen as a completely immoral, wanton slut, I tell you. She wanted to make sure everyone knew that. Her act was all purposeful. She unreservedly accepted and welcomed the touches of those men; and she encouraged them to be even bolder with her; taking Johnson's hand in her hand and reaching his fingers down low, very, very low; until she had his fingers lower than the lowest hair's breadth of her transparent, flimsy tissue-gauze barrier. Once there, she canted her legs slightly and used her hand to hold herself open while inserting Johnson's fingers into her vagina. And then she performed these slow motion-like, sensual thrusts on Johnson's fingers while she took deep, sighing breaths, laid her head upon Jim's shoulder, rolled her eyes heavenward and smiled the most beguiling, sinful smile I've ever witnessed. Johnson and Burnette obliged her performance. Burnette

continued fondling her breast and squeezing her derriere. With his free hand, Johnson made do by squeezing her other backside cheek.

"Now, you would think that at least one man would register disgust at her goings on. You would think that one of our husbands would sneer, turn his head away from her display, and say: 'She's just a whore.' But, not one man did. No, Millie. They all stood there; entranced, and spellbound, like dogs salivating at the prospect of mating with a bitch dog in heat. They were obsessed with her.

"I wondered for an instant, whether she gave any thought to her risk that one of the wives, perhaps myself, might step forward into her near circle and slap her. But then I had a sobering realization. We women were all like docile sheep, watching helplessly as if a lioness had inserted herself into our midst and was unconcernedly pleasuring herself, and ignoring our sensitivities. It occurred to me in a sudden chilling realization that our human lioness was not alone.

"She was figuratively surrounded by a hundred adoring male lions. Spellbound, they had fixated their adoring, approving attentions on her lascivious passion show. Suddenly, I had no doubt that, had one among us female sheep stepped into her performance circle and tried to interrupt her spectacle, dozens of male lions likely would have pounced upon that foolhardy woman; torn her limb from limb and shredded her entrails into a thousand pieces.

"It was plain to me that this Marty whore had ignited our men's animal lusts. She had them smitten and dazzled. She knew exactly what she was doing. Those men were salivating with whore-lust for ever more of the bitch's antics. Their imaginations were unbridled, as if they were transported to another time and place, far back into ancient history and Pagan prostitution worship times. I could feel their urges, those palpable hormonal urges, that she had imparted to these men. She had captivated them. She was controlling them with her innate, uncommon quality of leadership. It radiated from

every pore of her body. It signaled that it was righteous and healthy to desire her; that there was no sin or evil in lusting for her.

"The men became like obedient children, eating candy from her hand; or perhaps more like disciples receiving some mystical life sustaining inner sustenance from their goddess. Every one of them became a man transformed; seeking to pay homage to her. Her cunt, obviously, was their focal point. They wanted to worship it; flock to it. They were undistracted by the other women present or the glitz offerings of the gala's vendors. They wanted to immerse themselves in her yearning porn star cunt. I felt this invisible force. It called them to come to her; come to her insatiable cunt, kneel before it; seek its shamelessly immoral purity.

"I imagined feeling the limbic compulsions of grown, educated, wealthy men. They wanted to abandon everything they had; all they knew and held dear. They were eager to throw their lives and their fortunes upon the altar of that porn star's God defiling, marriage wrecking cunt. They all, in that ethereal state which she held them suspended, embraced their illusory closeness with her immoral persona. She understood how to perform; how to elicit the most immoral cravings in men. All men present, to a man, sought to partake of intimacy with her welcoming, glorious, triumphant cunt. Vicariously, every man left his woman for Marty. Vicariously, every man had sex with her; some even imagined marrying her. I departed the gala that night having no doubts about her threat to our way of life.

"That night I had trouble sleeping. I could not reconcile what I witnessed and felt with what my life's teachings and experiences had made me believe what I believed. I wondered: what was it that had caused this Marty woman to behave the way she did? What was it about her inner self that allowed her to do what she did? Where did she find the confidence to do what she did? And what was she drawing upon that allowed her to exude such confidence in her promiscuous performance and lead our men into their state of

adoring compliance with everything she did? How was it that men were naturally attracted to her the way that they were, like so many negatively charged iron filings suddenly glommed onto a positively charged anode? What made that happen? And why had it happened so quickly?

"I awakened with a start and my answers to my questions. My answers came to me like a strike from a lightening bolt. I realized that what I had seen was the returned to life reincarnated soul of a Pagan temple whore, perhaps Astarte herself, in the body of Marty. I instantly understood that I had witnessed a recreated preliminary foreplay to a prostitution worship rite. Marty was the life into which a soul had come back to us from across ten past millenniums! Her DNA carried the essence of religious whoredom within it! That explained why she could cavort so unconcernedly! It was all natural to her! Her world, or the world from which she carried her essential DNA and transported it to our world, considered what she did with those men the night before was all perfectly normal and natural!

"Marty was bringing all of us who watched her back to the way the world was in the time of Baal worship, into that time before the Judeo-Christian ethic was fashioned by men! I had my epiphany. Everything I witnessed was merely the natural order of change taking place. It was as common to our human experience as the Earth changing back its magnetic poles to the way they were configured many millenniums ago. And then epiphany after epiphany followed my first!

"Marty is a harbinger of our world's coming changes. People are forsaking the dogmas of their religions because their worlds have fallen apart, their families have disintegrated and all the foundation grounds upon which they had built their lives are shifting, shaking and unstable. They are looking to find new beliefs that make more sense to them and which are more understanding and relatable. And porn stars and their performed pornography are not immoral or bad

in this newly referenced world. They are as natural a phenomenon as Earth's changing magnetic poles. They have appeared before us to lead us in a new world, in ways that work for our society to survive and move forward.

"These beautiful, courageous women are not to be shunned and ridiculed. We must accept them, even venerate, and love them for the valuable work they do and the beautiful living art and pleasures they bring to us. Porn stars are simply modern-day goddesses. We must appreciate them. They bring refreshing relief from societal madness to all of us. Pornography, as I understand the world now, cannot be evil. It is a goodness and a beautiful, blessed relief from our dishonest, corrupt society and its intolerable stresses. I awakened and looked upon the world with fresh, more understanding eyes. I accepted Marty. Yes, Millie. I accept her. I no longer feel that I have some right to judge her. I want to know her better and become her friend.

"Face it, Millie. She upstaged all of us. She turned our ballroom floor into her impromptu adult film set. Even Evelyn confessed to the power of what she saw. Watching Marty fucking Johnson's fingers; shamelessly bringing herself to orgasm like she did, made Evelyn wet her panties. Our interloper whore is unnaturally, stunningly beautiful, and unnaturally certain of the rightness of her immorality and justification for it. She's a human mortal like the rest of us, of that I 'm certain; but I think she lives a life of reaction to some stresses of her own, from which she seeks to escape.

"And she must draw men into her orbit, for it is her liaisons with men that enables her to escape. Thus, she plays her vixen's game with men's hearts and, I am certain, their penises; but all of that is to mask over some inner need. And her need is strong. It drives her. There is no depth of immoral depravity into which she will not plunge to capture and strengthen her lascivious immoral liaisons.

"The mere act of her straightening herself up, the purposeful way she arose to present herself when Ed came and stood before her, seemed to mock the ordinariness and disposability of the rest of the men. She seemed of a suddenly different mindset and essence of herself; much like a butterfly leaving its dull confining cocoon behind and fluttering on to a better world for itself.

"It's her uncanny ability to leave the now and plunge into her new immersion realm of mystical transcendence. We witnessed her transformation. In this new psychic state, she has the uncanny ability to attract and seduce. The rest of us could not go there with her. It's a world unique to her. We could only observe this change in her. It was an elevation of the base tendencies in her soul to an even higher level of baseness; or perhaps I can better describe it as a deeper level of baseness.

"There was something taking place in all the men while her seduction of Ed was happening; something that they were very much aware of. It hushed them. It frightened all of them as well and made them stand aside, as if a dominant black wolf stepped into the presence of lesser wolves. They knew they were powerless to challenge Ed for the possession of her tempting favors. But their fascination with her and her seemingly inscrutable obsession with seduction held them captive to watch what she might do next. They knew they were about to see something rare. They were held spellbound by this horribly indecent, ravishingly beautiful, majestic woman.

"Oh, yes, Millie, Marty is a blatant, incorrigible whore all right. She was not about to hold herself back and stop then. And the men watching this could sense that. She was just getting started. She may as well have had a megaphone, announcing that she was open for business. No, she is not from white trash, Millie. She's driven by something more than money. She's from very serious big money. She's rich in her own right. Her mother is a partner at Sustack's. I could tell you a few things about her mother. Yes, her mother's the

one who married Joseph Maloney! I know the mother. She's a whore, too. The mother is more discreet about her whoring that the daugh- ter. But that mother is one of the biggest whores in town."

Unbeknownst to the gossips that had seen Marty's titillating dis- play, during Marty's performance, Miss Iniquity had experienced a sudden panic attack. Her early warning antennae had sensed that Marty's core magma, her latent nymphomania, was bubbling up and about to explode like a super volcano. She feared Marty would listen to Miss Promiscuity and Miss Shameless and abandon every inhibition. She foresaw Marty ripping away her garment and fall- ing into a marathon orgy spectacle with those hundred admiring, sex-obsessed men, right before the entire crowd and their wives. She dreaded that Marty's market value would then plummet; and she'd be stigmatized by this affluent crowd as an unworthy barn- yard pig, instead of being appreciated as a highly desirable, highly priced whore. She needed to rescue Marty from herself. The situa- tion was rapidly spinning out of control.

Quickly without forewarning, Miss Iniquity grabbed her two sister voices, held them close to her and cupped her hands over their two mouths. Safely silenced now and unable to interrupt her, Miss Iniquity talked sensibly to Marty's mind. She forcefully inserted herself into Marty's thoughts and launched into her soliloquy:

'Let them know you're a new kind of woman. You're not some- one who will cook, clean, and pick up after a man, nor will you suf- fer a man's pathetic misogyny or tawdry jokes, nor will you tolerate his boorish drunkenness and cries over his slights in life. Let all of them know that men are on earth for one reason only. They are here to please you, provide for you and lavish you in every conceivable luxury that they can afford to give you. Inform them that their little joy sticks exist for your pleasures to use as you please and put away when you choose.

'Listen! Can you hear their whispers about your mother? Yes, it's true. You are not the compliant docile daughter of your father, Joseph. No, you are not. You started out that way at WEX; but you have become much more like your mother, Susan. You're a sexual predator now. And, like your mother, you prey on men.

'Every bone in your body is the rigid spar of a calculating whore. Every bone is steeped in a primer of sin that reaches down into your marrow where it marries your DNA; and your iniquitous whore spar frame is well protected by many polished layers of your imper-vious immorality. Nothing will ever change you. Overlain upon your incorrigible bones is your mouth-watering, enticing flesh. All these men yearn to embrace you and love you. Mother and you are alike that way; but you are different kinds of whores, too.

'Mother became a whore to please Marvin and make more money. Your motive was to reclaim the love you lost when Father died. You substitute sex for the love you never got from Mother. Mother approaches her service work as an enjoyable duty; but prostitution is your first and only love. Making new conquests and seducing new lovers is your driven passion.

'Let these men know that they are welcome to your body, for a price, IF you choose to be with them. Make sure they know that a man can love you and you will love him back, but he must first understand your price is extremely high. He must understand that you will wrap him in your arms like a squid holds its prey until you have sucked his money life from him and left him a shell of the man he was before he loved you. He must understand that you are his femme fatale; that your methods will likely destroy his marriage and his family too; and that that is part and parcel of your bargain. Never feel sorry about the money you take from him. These men are wealthy. Don't let them cry about money.

'He must know that those are your terms. There can be no other way if he wants your love. He must completely commit to you with

no other considerations or remorse. And he may never complain or whine about your price, even when he knows you are also fucking his best friend, or his worst enemy; or his brother, boss, neighbor; or even his own son. He must know you are incorrigibly immoral and that you respect no boundaries. He must know that he may never set limits for you. And, yes, he'll pay yet another price. He'll discover that later.

'His mind will never be the same after he's loved you. When you are away from him, he will imagine what you are doing in the arms of another man. He'll realize then that he'll never change you. If he fantasized that he could change you when he fell in love with you, you will disabuse him of that notion. Whether he cares about you or not, whether he loves you or hates you for your behaviors afterwards will be his choices, but he will know what you do when you are away from him. His thoughts of you will stay in his blood and his blood will not lie. It will constantly remind him who you are and what you do.

'Finally, he'll accept your immoral whoring behavior and he'll return to you again and again, whether he hates you or loves you for what you are. He'll make his payment for another hour with you when he can afford you. Yes, your price is high, but once he's loved you, he'll know satisfying his addiction to you will be worth your price. Never compromise on your price. You are not here tonight to give yourself away for free!'

"Big Ed de Vere," continued the third female gossip, *"the billionaire who runs that network of safari, guiding, and hunting supply companies, had been eyeing her goings on. He must have liked what he was seeing. It was like he could read her mind; like the two of them had mental telepathy. No, Ed never got married. Yes, that's him, the tall one that consorts with whores and writes love sonnets about his liaisons with them. Whores fascinate him. No, Ed doesn't want a decent woman. He has no use for them. We've had him as a house guest several times and introduced him to Anna, Margie,*

Kathy, and Jane. They're all pretty, eligible, decent women. But Ed never even offered to drive them home. He went home by himself and then called over one of his whores. Ed loves whores; told me that they are humanity's true free spirits. He adores them; obsesses over the ways their minds work and their sexual predilections; especially the ones who go in for oral sex. There's no changing him. We gave up on changing Ed long ago.

"Well, Evelyn said Ed watched Marty sway her body and roll *her sexy brown peepers up into the tops of her eyelids until only her whites showed. That savoring pleasure look fascinated Ed. Not many women can throw their irises up under their eyelids like that, like they're experiencing an orgasm. He must have visualized featuring her ribald displays in his next big game calendar. She stood before Ed, cavorting with her bevy of lesser hunters, tempting Ed to approach her. These other men were kissing her like lap dog sycophants. They were hugging her, promising to take her on various hunts.*

"I watched Ed's eyes drink in her body. She doesn't have a skinny twig model's body for hanging dresses on; and it's not some chunky hint of what was once beautiful, either. That body is in its peak years for sex. It's a sensational, mouth-watering male bait body, complete with male catching facial accents. Even her bone structure signals sex. She's got those long, graceful bones. But not skinny or overly slender; perfect, showgirl like. Her eyebrows animate her face when she speaks. They rise with her smiles and tease inviting signals to the men who swarm around her. That angelic face and her heart shaped lips, those up-thrusting breasts, and hips remind men that we women are creatures they're privileged to fornicate with. Sex exudes from every pore of her body. I'm serious, Millie. She's a death sentence to our way of life!"

Second female gossip, whispering breathlessly: *"Evelyn heard her say:*

'I feel wonderful knowing I'm appreciated. I hate being alone, all by myself, with no one to have fun with. I'm so happy to meet all of you. I've never met any big game hinters before. Hunting those animals sounds so exciting and adventurous! I hope I can come along and watch how you hunt them, some day.'

"Her smiles and pleasure squeals fascinated Ed. He finally came forward through the crowd. He stared at her with his hungry wolf stare; like he was seeing a distressed rabbit held in the clutches of foxes. Everyone knows Ed is the club's alpha male. When he stepped boldly through the circle of men and stood before her, the breed lust of a stallion was in his eyes. Adoration! I saw it. He was smitten. His chest revealed his quickened breath.

"Evelyn said she never saw a man's eyes get as wide as that. She said Ed's eyes got lust wild, like a stallion's get when he's about to climb onto a mare. It seemed like Ed wanted to plant his face in that whore's vagina; devour her, right there in front of all the rest of us. He wanted her like a crazed man that wants something really bad."

Another voice, the voice of Goody, Miss Congenial Good Behavior, a voice Marty rarely heard, spoke to her when Ed first appeared:

'You're playing with fire, girl. He may decide you're undermining the dignity of the club. Don't be surprised if he takes your bottom over his knee and spanks you; then sends you home in a cab. Be prepared for that. He just might do it. You should stop your behavior and act like a lady'

But, Misses Promiscuity, Shameless, and Iniquity quickly muzzled Miss Goody. In unison they shouted down her plea for propriety:

'Get back to your knitting, prude. We've done our homework on Ed. We know he has a reputation for whoring. He loves the wild side of life; the wilder the better. This is no time to hold back.

'Marty, this is your golden opportunity. Put your wares out there on a sliver platter,' coached Miss Shameless. 'Show ardor. Entice him, draw him in. Make him salivate. Kiss him, and while you are kissing him, imagine how wonderful you'll make his cock feel when you have it inside your vagina. Imagine how you'll move your hips and tease the top of his shaft while he comes into you.

'Imagine all those moments when you'll be driving him wild. Imagine what your orgasms will be like with him. When you kiss him, imagine only those beautiful things that will happen for the two of you, when you make love. Summon your reservoir of tempting guile as only you can do. Let your impulses guide you. Return his interest with passion. Arrange to be alone with him as soon as possible; then make love like tomorrow will never come. Surely you can make him fall in love with you. He's a man. How could he not?'

Second female gossip, continuing: "Evelyn said Marty recognized Ed and greeted him by name. She obviously did her homework on our club. She blushed redness when she saw him, betraying her desire for intimacy. She raised her chin in a pleasing motion, stepped forward and away from her fondlers to fully offer all of herself only to Ed. She retreated her shoulders, thereby lifting her chest purposely to capture Ed's attention, as if offering up her cherry nipples for his appetizer.

"That convinced Evelyn that Big Ed was the one she intended to meet all along. Her whole face beamed angelic innocence and the duality of her coquettish, radiant smile. Her entire focus became Ed. She telegraphed that she believed that Ed was her hero man, coming to rescue her from all the lesser men. And, like savory butter, she sought to lavish all her warmth and femininity upon him. I swear I intuited that her heart leaped. Evelyn opines that the woman is nothing more than a calculating tart; and her pussy cat in a tissue dress act was just a ruse to attract big Ed and make him jealous-hot for her.

"Evelyn says there's much more to her than meets the eye. Lots of clever scheming goes on behind those sexy, soft brown eyes, said Evelyn. Nothing about Marty is an innocent accident, like she pretends. And there is no one that she relies upon. There's not true permanence in any of her relationships. She loves all her lovers; even collects them like fish on a string. But she trusts none of them with her decisions for her life. Evelyn said Marty had to know beforehand that multi-billionaire Ed was her first-class ticket into whoredom's paradise. Evelyn claims that's what her gala show was all about. She targeted Big Ed. And she got him."

LOVER ED

'Why, hello Big Ed! What a pleasant surprise!' Marty's sultry drawl was as coyly accessible and suggestively inviting as fresh creamery butter to a thirsty hot biscuit. Ed melted like butter. He acted like a puppy with its mouth agape, hoping she'd pick him up, hug him and adopt him. If he'd had a tail, he would have wagged it wildly. Her eyes beamed into Ed's like beacons welcoming a lost ship to enter her safe harbor. As she fluttered her long black eyelashes, she implored Ed: *'Won't you please join me?'*

"*She smiled a most tantalizing smile, Evelyn said, like she was coaxing an anxious puppy to jump into her lap. Ed intuited her intentions. That's when his mind left him. Evelyn said his eyes flared like there were sparks of fire coming out of them. She said Ed was consumed by her beauty. This proud handsome man suddenly lost all his power. He nodded his head like an obedient child. He started behaving irrationally, willing to throw away everything he had and doing whatever she asked; hoping to please her. Evelyn watched the two of them. she said she became spellbound. She saw Ed suddenly go crazy with thoughts of possessing her. She became the only thing that mattered to Ed. He stood, like a man bewitched, before that brazen unapologetic hussy.*

"He cleared his throat and said to her, real gentlemanly like:

'Miss, I notice your most enticing feature appears to be presently lacking for attention. Might I please offer my assistance?'

"Well, Marty didn't miss a beat. She batted her dark, love me, love me, eyes and told Ed that she'd very much appreciate his attentions. She became incredibly shameless and bold. She took Ed's hand; held his huge, weathered palm against the lily-white flesh of her lower stomach. She giggled from his hand touch. Clearly, his hand on her whoring belly pleased her greatly. She knew exactly what she was doing. Such a tease! She signaled Ed that she was about to lead his hand on a short journey down to her vagina. She smiled into Ed's eyes the most sinful 'Please come fuck me' smile Evelyn ever saw on any woman's face. She gave her hips a slight, suggestive twist to let Ed know he could have her body for his personal treat. Then, as I expected she would, she held her hand over Ed's hand and guided it lower, gently pushing it below her tummy; and then still further down, all the way down; until she had maneuvered it inside the low-cut plunge bottom of her disgusting tissue-paper dress. Then she held Ed's hand firmly in place right where she wanted him to keep it, firmly on her vagina. She didn't care one hoot about what anyone thought of her antics."

'Is this where you'd like to assist me, Ed?' she asked.

"Then she moved his hand up and down, holding his hand firmly over her vagina. While she did that, she smiled this salacious devil-may-care smile of hers. It telegraphed that she loved feeling Ed's touches there.

'I hope you'll assist me there, Ed. I'd love to be a very naughty girl with you,' she told him. 'Won't you, please, assist me?' she cooed. 'Won't you help me be a naughty girl? A naughty girl needs a man whom she can be naughty with, don't you know?' she asked, in that teasing, sultry voice of hers.

"She lifted her face toward Ed's. Obviously, she wanted to be kissed. She knew his kiss would be an endorsement of her behavior. She also wanted Ed to stimulate her, finger her vagina, right there in front of all those other men. She flaunted how immoral and shameless she was. There's nothing modest or ladylike about her. She knew exactly what she was doing the whole time, said Evelyn. She turned our annual gala into her personal sex show; like our whole gathering was being put on for her benefit; like we were throwing this extravagant coming out party for this promiscuous, attention seeking porn star. She didn't care what anyone thought of her goings-on.

"Evelyn said Ed put his arm around that small waist of hers and kissed her right then and there, while he massaged the inside of her vagina, stimulating her with his two fingers. YES, Dorothy, you heard what I said. He took over what Johnson was doing, just a short while before. Evelyn said it was like watching a big wolf run off a smaller one. Ed just held her in his arm while he fingered her, right there in front of everybody. Oh yes, she loved it. She was obnoxious about encouraging it this time. She brazenly moved her pelvis demonstrably back and forth over his fingers; like she was really enjoying the stimulation. Her eyes swooned in the way she does that thing she does with them. Her irises went behind her upper eyelids. All you could see where the whites of her eyes. She mouthed some words. I think she said: 'Oh, Ed, that feels wonderful!' in that dreamy voice of hers; while moving her pelvis to capture all the stimulation she could. It was like she'd done this sort of move a hundred times before; like she'd practiced it for her porn films. It was incredibly wanton. But it was also beautiful. I'll never forget what I saw. She literally made her vagina dance on Ed's fingers.

"YES, Dorothy. I know what I saw. I'm not making this up. No Dorothy, she didn't try to stop Ed. She encouraged him. She kept it up and kept it up; all the while she was kissing him and then, she reached out and found his cock through his pants and began stroking

it. She loved it, Dorothy! I could tell that getting Ed interested in her vagina was exactly what she wanted, all along."

'Ed,' she whispered, 'you have no idea how badly I want you to put your cock inside me. I've waited so long for this moment. I can't wait to be in bed with you. I'm starting to come, just thinking about it.'

"Some in the crowd gasped when they realized what those two were doing. But knowing the rest of the world was watching his carefree whoring didn't bother Ed. Both he and Marty had this fuck crazed animal lust look in their eyes. They were like dogs; a dog fox with his breeding vixen. Marty's eyes swooned again. Her irises disappeared into her upper eyelids.

"It was like a scene right out of a porn movie. It was erotically serene. Her eyeballs showed all white while Ed stimulated her vagina. She seemed to be in some other world. Maybe she was, Evelyn wasn't sure. She said her body seemed to be living in its own other world; loving all of Ed's stimulation. Evelyn said it was a sight to behold, like she was watching two lovers, frozen in time.

"That's when Ed asked her if she'd like to be photographed at his ranch. He said he wanted to dress her in exotic leopard skins, and then capture her smiles while showing off her vagina in erotic poses. He wanted her posed in seductive positions on his animal skins and hides. He said:

'I want photos of your vagina gushing semen, my semen, on all my skins and hides; grizzly bear, zebra, elk, moose, buffalo, giraffe, polar bear, leopard, and lion, every single one of them. I want to declare to the world that your vagina is more important than everything I ever did and everything I have. I also want playfully naughty photos of you posing with my stuffed snakes.'

"Marty purred and said yes to all his requests:

'Why, of course, I'll pose for you, Ed. I'll spread my legs and hold my vagina open for you, in every setting and every position you want.'

"*After she said that, Ed sprang his invitation. He invited her to join him on a two-week African safari. He arranged it so that he could kill both the world's biggest elephant and the world's biggest giraffe on the same trip. He wanted an explicit photo series of her stimulating her breasts and vagina, blowing kisses to the camera while posing on top of some huge bull elephant that he promised to kill for her. Then he wanted several shots of her in erotic poses. He said he wanted her and her glorious vagina to showcase the beautiful essence of perversity.*

"*He wanted to feature her sitting on the head of his trophy elephant, her legs spread widely with huge gobs of semen oozing from her vagina, flowing onto his elephant's head; demonstrating her vagina's supremacy; capturing the psychological imagery of her erotic immoral life's glorious triumph over all other non-human life forms; like her vagina dared anyone or anything to challenge its demands to be coddled, honored, and pleased.*

"*The message imagery being that this unfortunate elephant's humble life dared to present a challenge to the supremacy of her willful promiscuity, and she had asked Ed to kill it for her. He wanted to highlight her dominion over this poor, innocent beast. He would take several series shots of her posed naked, on top of this elephant, flaunting her semen gushing vagina in this same way, while she smiled, kissed, and sucked several cocks, captured their semen on her lips, licked her lips and stimulated herself while blowing kisses to the camera. He said he wanted to make a bold statement; his statement being that humanity was superior to the greatest of the other animals; that we had dominion over them; and that Marty's spectacular whoring vagina reigned superior over the entire world.*

"*He also wanted photos of her posed holding her vagina open, while smiling and sitting upon the elephant's trunk; and the same photo theme while she sat upon on its three-foot-long penis, but holding its tip to her mouth, as if she contemplated performing oral sex with it.*

"He also wanted scandalously naughty, erotic poses of her touching the tip of his giant giraffe's two-foot-long tongue to her vagina.

"She replied without a second's hesitation:

'Of course, I would, Ed. I'll do whatever you ask. How did you guess that I love oral sex?' Obviously, she was not put off in the least by the vilest, perverse images of craven debauchery. I could only accept this in my own mind as the awakening of the pagan soul that lives somewhere inside her, coming to us from millenniums past; freely expressing itself and joyfully, with clear consciousness, doing the sorts of barbarous things our pagan ancestors may have done.

"Morality codes were different then. I knew that much from the records of human sacrifices that they did. And I supposed that they did many other things that, while unthinkable to us today, were normal fare for them. I could not help but wonder: If Ed had asked Marty to murder a baby by throwing it into a raging fire, would she do so with a clear conscience? I thought, if she knew she had no risk of getting caught doing it, she likely would do that, too, as she seemed to care only about her own narcissistic pleasures. And then I thought further still and asked myself whether the modern-day abortions of fetuses greatly differ from what the pagans did with their unwanted babies; and I suppose, not so much. Are we really any different? As I said, Millie, I sought to understand Marty; not condemn her. I think humanity, for all its purported refinements, is still morally base and unchanged.

"No, Millie, Marty did not slap Ed. You're just not getting it Millie. Marty loved these perverse ideas. That's how much of a whore she is. She pressed her body against Ed's and she kissed him, all the while rubbing his cock; deliberately working her hand, long and patiently slow, like she was savoring the thought of posing for his debauched themes. She batted her eyes at him and kissed him a huge French kiss!

It was her whoring way of saying her welcoming 'yes;' and, definitely, her enthusiastic whoring, 'yes' to all of Ed's kinky fetishes.

"It was her way of telling Ed she'd gladly be a totally immoral, debauched whore for him. She was, I have no doubt, also visualizing the publicity these stunts would create for her. She'd possibly be doing the most debauched things any woman had ever done. Like a totally unrestrained whore! A completely uninhibited, immoral whore! A ribald whore without one scintilla of decency! None! None, at all!

"Evelyn swore Marty was quietly experiencing an orgasm right there in front of everyone while Ed was proposing those photo shoots and fingering her. Evelyn believes the thought of Ed killing exotic animals and placing her on them, like he was honoring her as the world's ultimate trophy, stimulated her blood lust and helped her come. Yes, Millie, it's true. Women like her can make themselves orgasm that easily. It happens in their minds, Millie. She also has that heart shaped upper lip. They say women with lips like that can orgasm really fast. They can make themselves squirt right off, like happy little water fountains.

"Then, she asked Ed what was in it for her:

'Tell me, Ed, what might a naughty girl get for posing her most naughty bad girl poses in all those photos?'

"He said he'd give her fifty thousand dollars; he'd have the giraffe's hide made into a custom luggage set for her and he'd give her one of the tusker's ivories. Now, my Bill knows those values. He said the luggage would be worth about thirty thousand dollars. And one tusk from a giant tusker is worth about three hundred thousand dollars. Ed offered over three hundred eighty thousand dollars to get provocative pictures of her glistening, creamy-like fleshed and smoothly waxed, butterfly tattooed vagina, in explicitly erotic poses; mocking the insignificance of those magnificent animals when compared to her wanton sexuality.

"Ed must have a case of lust madness, Millie. He intends to elevate that shameless whore above nature's majesty. She's as bad as he is, Millie. Some whores will do anything for money. She'll go to Africa and mock those beautiful animals. That breaks my heart. Those two are well suited for each other. Well, yes, I understand mounting a trophy on a wall mocks that animal's life, too, but what she and Ed are going to do seems different to me somehow. It's gross.

"Yes Millie, I know we are animals, too; but this is different. Killing an animal to glorify a whore like that; and knowing she's cheerfully going along with it; no qualms or moral reservations about it; well, it just turns my stomach. There's nothing this whore won't do, Millie. There's something buried deep inside the character of that woman. Behind her image of sex goddess there's some deeply rooted trouble bothering her, I could feel it. I believe her conscience would not be troubled over murdering humans either. None whatsoever. And I think she'd mock their lives, too. I think that woman would do anything to slake her blood lust and her craving for money.

"Nothing that immoral woman does would ever surprise me. I'd bet she likes to do bondage and kinky sadomasochism stuff, too. I got the distinct sense that this woman will do anything. NO, Millie, I'm sure you'll never get her into a church. She has no use for religion. No, I'm not even going to approach her about it. It would be a waste of time. She has no morals whatsoever, none at all. I almost feel sorry for her. There must have been past trauma in her life.

"Ed said he'd showcase full sized photos of her vagina in the big game calendar that he gives away to his millionaire clients. He wants to add little quotes by each trophy animal photo, like:

'My pussy lips were thrilled by this hunter. Watching him kill his lion made me all wet inside.,' and, 'I loved making love with the man who bagged this one. I had to let him take me, too. What a man! I loved how he came deep inside me; how he dominated me!'

"He said he wanted many additional photos with cum oozing from her vagina, too. She smiled a big smile when she heard that. Obviously, that signaled her that Ed intended to fuck her, probably often; and probably with some of his guides and other hunters, too. The thought of being treated to an extravaganza of cocks in Africa's wilds obviously pleased her.

"While she listened to Ed's ideas, I saw her business brain kick in. She didn't just say yes to Ed right away. She clever and astute. She wanted one additional condition met before she agreed to Ed's proposal. She flattered Ed; told him she heard he was a terrific lover. But before they went to Africa; before she spent all those nights alone with him, she wanted to find out for herself. She asked him:

'Ed, word came to me that you are a terrific lover. I was wondering if I could confirm for myself if that's really true? I know it's forward to ask you this, but could I come to your ranch and spend an evening with you, before we trot off to Africa? I want to prepare myself for everything you'll want from me. I want to make you happy Ed.'

"I admired her for that. She knows how to turn the tables on a man, put a man in his place. She wanted to be sure she'd be safe with him; no rough stuff. She doesn't just give her vagina away. She's a good businesswoman. She puts a sky-high price on her prized asset.

"Well, Ed's face lit up like moonbeams on sunshine when she asked him that, like he saw his soul's redeeming miracle. Ed acted like he'd lost his mind completely. He looked like he went star-struck, lust-crazed, head over heels insane in love over that whore. Yes, right there in front of everyone, as if the rest of the world didn't matter at all. He knelt humbly before her, as if he needed to pray to God; then he stretched that low bottom cut in her dress even lower, until her entire vagina was revealed.

"Yes, he did that. Right there it was, boldly exposed, out in the open air, before all those men and God himself. Evelyn saw it too.

She said she thought she was watching some erotica film; but that blocked out patch that the censors place over the woman's delta spot was absent. There was her shameless, wanton vagina right before Ed's face, like it knew it was the center of attention; and like it had this mind of its own and it held the entire room in its power. Marty gave a chortling laugh when he did that, like she was letting him know she was thrilled by the way he exposed her.

"That's when Ed placed his hands upon her ass and brought her vagina right up to his lips, like he was a reverent priest beholding the sacred offertory chalice. Evelyn said Ed acted surreal, like he was suddenly afflicted with insanity. He was completely under the powers of that whore, like she was possessing him; and he was having an out of body experience. Evelyn said Ed acted like he'd go berserk and kill everyone if he couldn't have her. It was like he had discovered a pagan's reverence for lust.

"Ed closed his eyes like he was overcome with reverential bliss, preparing himself to taste his portion of his goddess's lust essence. Before their entire gathered congregation of big game hunters, Ed drew his head closer to her vagina until he touched his lips to it. It was like he was blessed to impart this kiss; like he was giving a sacred kiss to his most sacred deity; like he was humbled to finally be worthy of touching his Holy Grail. He then held his lips against it for the longest time, as if he had finally discovered his true spiritual home; and now he was blessing his transformational host, binding his soul to it. I knew I was witnessing a moment of spiritual adoration. Ed was experiencing his 'come to his goddess' moment.

"This was an induction process. Ed's allegiance to Marty's whoring was creating this unshakable psychological bonding to her. I felt his allegiance taking hold. He seemed to be asking some unseen deity to remove his newfound devotion, to take her away from him, if his fervent passion was not meant to be; but his newfound deity did not remove herself from him. She stayed in place. She placed

her hands upon his head, thus assuring him that he was welcomed into her kingdom of iniquity. I witnessed Ed's new god approve him and command him to worship her. His new vagina god kept herself right there; kept her vagina steadily pressed against Ed's lips; kept her hands upon his head as if she was giving him the sacrament of baptism into her world of whoredom and her invitation to receive her eucharist at the same time. Marty rotated her hips toward him, seemingly to push her vagina even harder against his lips, as if she was confirming the sacred rightness of what they were doing.

"I saw this chimera-like image of Marty's butterfly tattoo, still partially concealed by her gauze tissue dress, attach itself to Ed's face; like it was taking Ed into its power and was fluttering away with his soul and his brains into some carefree paradise world. Obviously, Marty loved what Ed was doing and all the attention he was bringing her, but there was more than that. It was a transformational happening.

"It was like some spiritual power willed that these two become joined. Ed felt compelled to commit himself to her. Marty stood there; confidently, like a spirit force within her was pleased; feeling glorified that she had an unrepentant wanton soul. She was oblivious to the rest of us; tuned us out; didn't care a hoot what we saw or thought. She smiled a pleased smile. She knew she had seduced her targeted man. Then, she beamed that same smile to the men around her, telling them that, in the fullness of time, she would seduce them too.

"She kept her hands firmly on Ed's head while he held his lips to her vagina, as if reassuring Ed that it was right and natural for him to remain with her; place his trust in her; not let anything or anyone deter him from holding his lips hard against her vagina. She was signaling her commitment to Ed's quest, which was to advance and champion her notoriety and glory:

'Why, Ed, it seems you are making my vagina your new religion! I'm honored with your conversion to the New Morality Standard.'

"Ed didn't speak. With deliberate, respectful devotion, he slowly kissed all around both sides of her sex, as if honoring his sin goddess's presence before us mere mortals. I watched Ed's epiphany. He was blessing all the whoring Marty had done in her promiscuous past and would undoubtedly continue doing in her future. It was as if, in this spiritual moment, Marty's fuck-happy vagina became Ed's sacred altar. He paid homage to it. He set it above and apart from the rest of the spellbound congregation. Our eyes became glued to the two of them. Everyone was silent. We stared. We were witnessing a man overcome with devotion.

"It was an uncommon spectacle. No one thought to sip their drink. Many of the men seemed envious of Ed. I could read that in their faces. They were like guest observers on a live porn set. That's when Ed's lips began delicately kissing her sex, everywhere; lovingly; adoring her lust craven lady bits. He blessed every inch of that woman's wanton vagina with the same tender-sweet loving kisses that one adoringly bestows upon newborn infants while wishing them all good things for their lives. Kissing her vagina like that, like it was something holy, seemed incomprehensible; yet Ed did it. He did it shamelessly and without hesitation or reservation. And it was beautiful. I swear, I thought I was being transported back in time to a temple worship service, where kissing the prostitutes' vaginas was a normal part of a sacred fertility ritual.

"Ed was completely absorbed in worshipping all the fornications that Marty did in her porn movies; honoring all the notorious sinning she'd previously done on screen and off screen with her Premium Membership partners. Ed was accepting, blessing, and honoring all of that. It's what he wanted for his own life! He lovingly kissed his lips to that whore's vagina, up and down its entire length, both sides of it, at least three times. I saw him do that with my own eyes, Millie.

"It was appalling, disgusting; a form of obsessive insanity; but it was somehow beautiful, deliberate and knowing awareness, too.

Ed was making his statement to all of us. He was leaving our world and converting his life to hers. He was kissing our contemporary religion and all our customs goodbye and kissing some form of Pagan creation worship hello. Marty and her nympho vagina was what he wanted more than anything else. I've never seen a man so smitten by a woman's vagina; never seen anything like that in my life. No, Millie, I'm not exaggerating. I wouldn't have believed it if I hadn't seen it all with my own eyes. It felt like I was witnessing the birth of a new cult religion. Evelyn saw it too.

"Evelyn commented how Ed paused noticeably between every kiss, before he continued his worship ritual. He went totally, mentally nuts over that whore's vagina. I've heard that some men can get that way over a vagina, but I never thought I'd live to see it. It was beyond weird. Different. Totally different from anything I ever knew or saw before. Ed was definitely into something spiritual. It was something way beyond lust. He was experiencing some kind of perverse reverence for that whore's vagina, and her whoring way of life. Maybe Ed was living a revenant return, some kind of renewal of his life, or having one of those out of body experiences. It was like the whole world stopped while the two of them did this…. this spiritual thing.

"Whatever charm Marty held over Ed; he was certainly appreciating it. And unashamed to show it. He savored her vagina. Evelyn said she had a revelation at that moment. She realized it was not so much that Ed adored that whore's vagina. Oh, he adored it, all right; but it was more that Ed was announcing to his legion of followers that the unapologetic whoring that this woman did; the kind of life she lived, moved him into a kind of pagan prostitution worship rapture state.

"Evelyn's husband, Rusty, saw it too. He said Big Ed acted like he was in a church confessing a loyalty covenant. Rusty said it was Ed's way of promising his new whore that he'd throw out all his old

whores. Ed seemed to be tying his love, honor, and fortune to this one special whore. Rusty says Ed knows he's got terrible morals. But Ed knows he can't live any other way. Rusty thinks Ed's got pagan blood in him. He doesn't want to live with our morals. He just can't do it. Ed's always lusted after whores. But now, this one got him smitten. Rusty believes Marty's got Satan's evil spirit inside her. He thinks her vagina possesses ungodly, sinful powers that controlled Ed and made him fall crazy in love, right there."

Heard only by Marty, when Ed began touching his lips to her vagina, her voices burst into chorus:

'Welcome him to receive you,' said Miss Shameless. *'Flex your rump cheeks. Nuzzle your vagina closely into his nose and lips. Open your stance slightly so he can taste your velvety petals. That's it! Now, roll your hips slightly. Let your scents signal that you love what he's doing.'*

'Ed is an alpha male, like Fred; but he's not like Fred in his style,' spoke Miss Promiscuity. *'Ed isn't neat. He's messy. Look at his mop of scraggly hair. It's washed and clean; but not brushed or combed. It's all Ed, all natural and all uncaring about what anyone thinks. In his own scruffy, scraggly way, he is wildly sexy, untamed, and strong; a mighty black wolf alpha male. He will fuck you with bursts of incredible strength and with powerful stamina that will send you to the heavens. He'll give you orgasms from the strength of his penis alone, without needing oral sex; but you'll have plenty of that as well, that's for sure.*

'He's a predator all right, but not like an eagle,' voiced Miss Iniquity. *'He's more like a bear; or better yet, a wolverine. He's afraid of nothing. He doesn't care what anyone thinks of him or what he does. He doesn't need to care. He has more money than any of the others. He does and takes whatever he wants. Let yourself and everything within you relax. Follow his lead. Go with him. Let him ravage you right here, right now, if that's what he wants. He has a reputation for*

loving whores. So, you be the most uninhibited, bold, brazen whore you can possibly be. Be totally self-serving!

'Let him hear your pleasure sounds, let him hear you saying: "Oh yes, Ed, that's beautiful. I love what you're doing, I love how you're making me feel," urged Miss Promiscuity. *'Use your hands to pull slightly upward at the back of his head and neck. Let him know you crave having his tongue inside your sex. Let him hear you moan to signal to him that you love cunnilingus; you love his tongue exploring your vagina. Let him know you feel as much animal lust as he does.'*

'Tell him you feel connected to him in a special way and you're honored that he selected you for his calendar,' prompted Miss Iniquity. *'Tell him all this posing for debauchery will be perfectly natural for you. Tell him you'd feel honored to work with him on his special projects. Tell him you'd love doing threesomes and orgies with him, too; and you'll happily make yourself available for his best clients' pleasure times between hunts.*

'Stay alert for business opportunities. Be good to him. Don't hold back. Show him that you love what he's doing; that you enjoy being an exhibitionist. Prove he can trust you to do as he pleases. You need to submit to him, like you are a deer being ravaged by a wolverine. Let him enjoy you. Encourage him. He'll love you from this moment onward, forever. This man will promote you and establish you with his top clients; and you'll make premium compensation. He'll ensconce you in a whore's nirvana. Love him with your whole heart.'

Second female gossip, confiding her thoughts and continuing:

"Ed became that Marty woman's supplicant that day. A kind of pagan religious happening went on inside Ed's head. After he honored Marty's salacious promiscuity, his hands parted her vagina like it was the divine host. Then, his tongue savored her, like he was drinking from the Holy Grail. He tongue-fucked her vagina right

there in front of everyone. It was like the two of them were making a porn flick. Then Big Ed stood upright to claim his prize. He lifted that whore right up off the ground; gathered her body tightly to his own and kissed her, boldly and long on her mouth.

"Ed willed himself to commit to that whore like Saint Peter committed himself to Christ. Ed became like Marty's devoted foundation rock. He's going to advertize her, like he's spreading the good word gospel. Knowing Ed, like I do, he'll spread her message far and wide, like religion. He'll proclaim that her vagina is the real deal! Ed will go all in for that whore. He'll convert new subjects to her cause and open new venues for her. Money will pour into her cash register; and with Ed promoting her wantonness, her cult of followers will multiply like the fishes of the Sea of Galilee.

"I fell off to sleep that night with that sense of the dynamic I had witnessed. Then I had this very strange dream. It was more of a flashback than a dream. It was as if my soul's spirit had awakened within me to remind me of my original, most primal, communal need; that need to believe in my rightful belonging place in the world; that belief in my own perpetuity; that expectation that I would give birth and life would renew; that the sun would return to us from its dark cold places to warm us again.

"Then I saw a dead wooly mammoth. It was so realistic and so large. I could see its dead eyes still looking at me; its gleaming tusks; the twenty spears that had been jammed into its hide to bring it down; and the blood streaming from its wounds. A group of about thirty people were walking and dancing around it. They had a fire going and one man was making rhythm sounds by beating on sticks. They were celebrating that they had killed this magnificent animal and that its body flesh would sustain them for a while. They were dressed in different sorts of animal skins and hides. Many carried spears as they danced and shouted their outbursts of triumph around the slain animal. One man had a skin in which he carried

obsidian rocks to flake into spear tips. Another man had a skin that carried sticks which made different sounds when he beat these sticks together.

"One of the women wore a distinctive tiger's skin. That set her apart from the other women who wore ordinary skins. There was a confident boldness about her. She was fearless; authoritarian; unashamed. Small bones with feathers attached protruded from her pierced ears. She was the dominant female of this group; and comely, shapely, beautiful. All watched her as she climbed up on the beast and sat upon its head, like that was her rightful place; her throne. Then, she held her vagina open and displayed herself. Then, one after the other, the men in the group climbed up to her, kissed her, and fornicated with her. Her orgasm fluid sprays joined with these men's semen flows from her vagina. This fluid stream poured out of her and onto the head of the dead beast. My dream mind grappled for an explanation of what I was seeing.

"Then it dawned on me. This pagan tribe understood that human life originated inside the female vagina. They were symbolically sending their blessings and thanks for their human lives into their goddess woman; and through her vagina, into the murdered beast by their orgasm flows; doing this ritual to enable the dead beast to receive their life's blessing which they were imparting to it; thus, ensuring that it would, in return, provide sustaining life to them when they ate its flesh! They fornicated on their kill to honor the animal's life and its blessings of life being given to them, through their consumption of its flesh!

"By fornicating with all the men of her tribe, Marty's ancestor bonded those men into a cohesively effective hunting group. She made their success possible by helping them think and behave cooperatively, as a group, instead of as individuals. They were stronger as a group. And as a group that came together and believed in each other through the sexual wonders of their pagan goddess, these

people loved each other, believed in each other, and sustained their lives.

"They appreciated that their Pagan goddess unified them. They believed that she was their source of strength and the salvation of their lives. They understood how much they needed her. If she told them to kill an enemy tribe, they would do that. If she told them to toss undesirable, unwanted children into their sacrificial fire, they would do that, too. They worshipped and adored her; and as a collective group, they all and every one of them, loved her. Her vagina was their only one true god. Their worship ritual on that slain woolly mammoth predated man's invention of gods in Mesopotamia and Egypt by at least a thousand generations. I dreamed that our modern-day Marty possessed this woman's same goddess power; that the woman on the woolly mammoth was one bookend to the human experience, and Marty was the other. And it is a continuum experience. Didn't Sara fornicate with Pharoah to amass fabulous riches? Didn't Bathsheba, Salome, Cleopatra, and Isabella all murder those who opposed their power? My sleep became troubled before I awoke. I wrestled with my question. Was Marty like that Pagan goddess? Was she like Sara, Bathsheba, Salome, Cleopatra, and Isabella? Would she murder her enemies? I think she would.

"When I awakened, I felt a frightening chill. I finally had my understanding of what had happened at the gala. Marty has returned to us the spirit soul of her pagan goddess ancestor who had lived several thousand generations before us. That same pagan spirit soul lives within Marty. Everything now made sense to me! Of course, she would readily agree to do those photos for Ed. It was perfectly natural for her spirit soul to say 'yes' to him. It's perfectly normal for her to unhesitatingly do many pornographic things which we modern humans label obscene. Those things are entwined within her spirit soul. They are the very essence of her. She uniquely

appreciates doing what is only natural for her to do. She yearns to display her promiscuity; always and everywhere. The men gathered around Marty were naturally attracted to her ribald display. Deep within their own spirit souls they intuitively understood that she was reliving a primal ritual. What she did resonated with their spirit souls. She enabled them to see life as it really is, on its primal needs-based level, stripped of mankind's invented rules and pretenses. She reprioritized our understandings to appreciate the vital necessity to honor and sustain human life. I now understand her in ways which I could not before.

"Our porn stars remind us of our deeply seated timeless need to honor life's creation. And they encourage us to perpetuate life. They bring us a message which is diametrically opposite the death-based messaging of misogynistic religions. The porn stars remind us of the natural artistic beauty of life's lovemaking creation process. Humanity needs their pagan message of life's glorious wonders. We need to appreciate nature's beautiful life creation method. Their work is both artistic and beautiful. It addresses our most deeply seated need; that foundation rock need to live and appreciate life. But what they portend for civilization as we know it is chilling.

"Religions arrived a thousand generations after my dream woman in her tiger skin fornicated on that mammoth's head. Religions address a need for social order. They took common sense dos and don'ts and codified them. Paganism, in its modern expressions of prostitution and pornography, is not incompatible with modern religions. But it is perceived as a threat to the established order. It acknowledges that humanity's foundation is built upon life, not death. It worships the need for life and life's continuity, upon which religions were first constructed. It must not be seen as a threat to religions.

"When understood in this light, there is nothing evil about prostitutes or porn stars. They are a beautiful and necessary part of our

social order. They link us to our natural past and provide continuity to social progress. We need not fear these wonderful marvelous women or castigate them. They are doing nature's work. Appreciate their message of life. Like our tribal warrior ancestors, we must embrace them, adore them, and love them. Uninhibited, they bring life and love to all of us. They are our modern-day pagan goddesses.

"We must idolize them for their reminder messages of the beauty of life; like the tribal goddess of my dream did for her people. Porn stars remind us to prioritize love and life. Love and life are our ultimate destinies. If we do not live for life, what else could possibly be worth living for? These glorious women are the vessels into which and from which we can reaffirm our belief in life and acknowledge our need to love and to live. In this sense they are forward looking and far seeing. Contrast porn stars' message of faith in humanity's future with the messaging of the arrogant, close-minded, nay sayers who fly their carbon barfing jets to Davos, Switzerland. Those know it all's tip-toe about in their rarified milieu like a herd of silly cats sniffing under each other's tails, while mewing how everyone else is destroying their personal planet. Ridiculous!

"The hypocrites are missing the big picture. Humanity is about to go to the stars! We are about to populate the universe! We need to create a huge reservoir of humans so we will have enough people to accomplish our destiny. We need many more humans; many more babies; trillions and trillions more humans; not fewer! We don't know how to get there? So, what! Someone figured out fire. Someone figured out air travel. Someone figured out electricity and nuclear power; and radio and television, and computers. Relax! There's harmonic frequency resonance in celestial bodies. Someone will figure out how to unlock that energy. Someone will figure out how to warp space and time. Travel to the far reaches of the universe will become instantaneous. Trust humanity. Someone always figures it out. Don't

obsess over minor details. Ignore the hand wringing tail sniffers. Our purpose here on Earth is to reproduce ourselves. We need to make more babies, not fewer; make more love, not less!"

First female gossip, also supportive of Marty:

"Yes! Marty's got it right! She was delivering a message. We just needed to see it. She was not vulgar, Becky. No, Becky, honestly, she wasn't. She was actually refreshing and beautiful. Your problem is you see everything as black or white, good, or bad. I'm telling you; it was neither. It was odd and immoral; but also, it was surreal, ethereal, and beautiful. Maybe it was even moral in a raw and honest kind of way. It was the birth of devotion love between a man and a woman. You just needed to see it for yourself; and you need to see things differently than you're used to seeing them. There, amidst all those exhibits of guns and dead animal trophies, that Marty woman whore showed those egomaniac killers that there was something more beautiful and more challenging in life than killing animals and mounting their heads on our walls.

"She showed those cretins the raw beauty of life. Many who saw what she and Ed did commented that they were beautiful together. She made sin look truly glorious and beautiful. Sin and lust are part of life, too, you know. And, done honestly and well, sin and lust kind of pull something out of me. When that happens, I feel a kind of love and it's beautiful to behold. It awakens different sensations in my mind.

"Yeah, Geraldine, she knows how to market herself. She wraps herself in sin and sells the package brilliantly. She shows us that sin can be beautiful, acceptable, and even normal. She blends sin with sex appeal and presents it with a kind of spellbinding intensity. It's romantic and transformative. She's a class act. It's like she's not actually a whore; more like she's some kind of goddess from another time and place. And, she's damn confident, certain of her sex appeal and

her moves. That confidence sets her apart from other women, even more than the way she flaunts her sexuality.

"How? Well, she reached through invisible psychological barriers to pluck love from the hearts of those rowdy men, didn't she? She tamed them. Think about that. One woman, and she tamed all of them. It's like they became her submissive, trained dogs. While she carried on with Ed, she transformed those hidebound killers into men who recognized a woman's sexual needs. Even if they didn't learn a damn thing, at least they saw it. There's always hope."

Third female gossip, weighing pros and cons:

"Yeah, maybe she did perform a kind of community service for the rest of us. But that woman is playing with fire. Just wait. Someday, one man will get all hot blooded over her. That'll be trouble. No telling what a man will do when he gets like that. I don't think she understands men at all. Some men don't like feeling some woman is using them for a play toy. She works men like she's the one in charge all the time. There are men that don't sit well with that.

"Marsha thinks this Marty woman could be our savior, some new kind of feminist leader who uses erotic film art as her venue. Marsha's been saying for years that it's time for us women to take over the world, because men have fucked things up long enough. She believes Marty figured how to use vagina lust against men to escape their domination. She believes Marty invented new battle of the sex's tactics to defeat men. Instead of being passive, instead of letting our men decide when, where, and how often they have sex with us, Marsha says we women need to become the aggressors. We need to tell men our terms. We need to demand more of them and make them try harder to satisfy us.

"She thinks all of us should become extra aggressive sexually, like Marty. Marsha's always making posters, going to protests, burning her bras and screaming about every cause imaginable. Now she's got herself all hot and lathered up over this new idea. This sex aggression

against men thing is a whole new direction for Marsha. She told me she's found her true self. Yeah, I agree with you. I also wonder what happens in Marsha's mind sometimes. I think she secretly wishes she could become an adult film star. She's got the body and face for it. She's really beautiful, but she hides her beauty under those thick black rimmed glasses and her baggy men's clothes. If she got her hair done, slapped on make up and changed her wardrobe, she'd be a knock out. Whatever goes on in Marsha's mind is complicated.

"I also heard from Jane a day after the gala. She said a rich Lakota Indian Chief attended and watched Marty's performance. He's got eleven casinos in the Dakotas, Montana, and Washington State. Well, Jane said he talked to Marty about modeling for some sex robots that he wants to put into his casinos. He wants her to make hologram sex videos, so the viewer feels like he's doing sex with her, right there live and in person. Then he wants to make life-like robots of Marty's body, program those robots with artificial intelligence to make sex freely available to his high rollers, and pair those robots with Marty's holograms. That way, he's thinking they'll have a better sex experience than with real live prostitutes, without all the costs and headaches of letting hookers working his casinos. Jane said Marty will get a royalty on the hours men use on the entire robot fleet. That Marty woman stands to make a fortune."

CHAPTER FOUR

As lookers-on feel most delight, that least perceive a juggler's slight, and still the less they understand, the more they admire (her) slight of hand. (Samuel Butler: Hudibras)

....; put thyself into the trick of singularity. She thus advises thee that sighs for thee. (Shakespeare: Twelfth night)

MANAGING LOVERS

"Ed? Oh yes, he still sees her," continued the third gossip. "Ed doesn't hold back. He's committed to her. She became his female Satan that day. Oh, yes, Becky. He totally surrendered his soul to her. He advocates for her life style now. He treats her like a new bride. They kissed long soul kisses, passionately wrapped in each other's arms. Ed loved what she was selling; couldn't get enough of it. People said the scene was touching, loving and beautiful. The two of them emerged from that spotlight into a world of their own. Marty's face showed admiration for Ed.

'Evelyn said she watched the two of them falling in love. Yes, she's sure it was real love. Marty's eyes smiled a fiendishly devil-lust look. She signaled Ed that she was eager to perform every imaginable debauched sex act that he could dream up. She asked how soon she could see him and when they'd take off for Africa.

"Evelyn said Marty has that effect on men. She quells their little boy fears, convinces them that they are worthy of love. She loves all of her lovers with her whole heart in that same way. They believe in *her. Because of her they believe in themselves. They believe they can do better, be better, and succeed at anything. Evelyn says that many of her lovers, even men who are married with kids, will swear that she is the love of their lives. She gives them purpose somehow. And they strive mightily to please her. Why? I can't begin to understand how she affects men like that. It must be that she honestly does love them and they can feel it in their bones. Nobody can fake love for long; not even a whore.*

"You're asking me how Fred handled her after she behaved like that. Oh, Becky, come on! You know Fred. Her behavior didn't bother him one bit. He was off looking at new guns and ammo and trying to put together some Tibetan Snow Leopard hunts. There are only five of those beautiful cats left in the world. They have spectacular, gorgeously thick fur. Fred intends to kill all five of them before anyone else can get to them. He wants to make another fur coat for her.

"Yes, I'm serious. He adores that whore. He has permits for China, Nepal, Tibet, India, and Afghanistan. He intends to exterminate their species so he can give her the world's softest, warmest, most luxurious coat. He loves pleasing her. Yeah, that's Fred. He gets single-minded focused on a goal. No, she didn't leave with Ed. She left the party with Fred. She always leaves with the man she arrives with. I heard that she thinks doing otherwise is immoral. Yes, she spent the night with Fred. Oh, I'm certain she fucked Fred that night. She's totally loyal to her dates and appointments that way. Yes, I'm certain she also loves Fred.

"I can't understand her either, Becky. Apparently, she's mentally capable of loving many different men at the same time. Just because we can't do that doesn't mean she can't do it. It fits with her nymphomania disease. Both Ed and Fred are thrilled when they are with her. Times have changed, Becky. Society accepts all sorts of behaviors now. In the past we were expected to help poor and unfortunate people; but now, we just look away from them,

like they don't exist. There are so many poor people; too many. They will always be there. And there will always be more of them. It's hopeless to try to help them. So, why even bother trying? They're losers. It's more mentally pleasing to pine over a porn star whore than to trouble your mind over hopeless people. It's more soothing to fantasize. Why give yourself headaches and anxieties when you can dream of having sex?

"There's no longer any stigma to being an erotic film actress, either. Things aren't at all like they once were. Men are actually proud to be seen with porn stars now. You should have seen how those men acted when they were around Marty. The more teasing and kissing and cock stroking she did; the more lewdness she displayed, the more they all wanted her.

"Yes, I agree. It bends my mind, too. Both Fred's and Ed's chests burst with pride when they have her on their arms. They're grown men, but they behave like proud dogs that have snatched a juicy bone away from the pack; and they never let go of her. Oh, yes, she always keeps them separated. No one sees her with both men at once. She's smart that way. Yes, Becky, I agree. She's made her nympho disease highly profitable. I understand, Becky. What do you expect me to do about it? They're all adults! I know, Becky, I'm frightened for my husband too. I know. Men are just dogs. There's no changing them. Let's get our minds off her. Let's get up a bridge game and have a nice lunch."

Third female gossip, with a fresh titillation:

"Mary Lou said that John took Marty to a gambling charity at a downtown hotel. Yes, Marjorie's John, I'm serious. Marjorie doesn't know about it, so don't tell her. Yes! She wore an indecent mini skirt and sat high on a table, her legs apart just widely enough to display her pink panties. She never wears a bra. Her nipples showed through her blouse. Molly noticed too. No, Sharon, it wasn't an accident. To understand her, Sharon, you can't be thinking the way we

do. Modesty is the furthest thing from her mind. She wears those transparent sheen panties on purpose. She intentionally gets men thinking about fucking her. That's what works for her.

"Molly overheard her conversation with John. Marty asked John if he missed having intimacy. Well, five minutes later he got a hotel room and they disappeared for two hours. John didn't return, but Marty did. This time she wore transparent white panties. Yes, her vagina showed through those, too. It would be impossible for a man not to see it. She trolls her bait for men that way. Who knows? John may have kept her pink ones as a souvenir. She's definitely got her hooks into John. I'm telling you. It's true. She must have learned that John has big money. Mary Lou says she learns all about a man before she marks him for her approach. She targets the man she wants.

"No, she is not indiscriminate, Sharon. She knows exactly what she's doing. YES, we have a problem. We have a top ranked adult film star running wild, unchecked in our social circle, attending all our parties and events, enticing our men and picking them off, one at a time. There's no difference in her behavior, whether she's on set making a film or whether she's socializing with our husbands. She's willing and ready to fuck, regardless of the setting or the circumstances. She doesn't even bother to make pretenses about what she's about. She'll even hit on a man right in front of his wife, like his wife isn't even there.

"You heard what happened to Olivia, haven't you? Oh, you haven't? Well, let me tell you. Her husband, Phillip, has four high-end restaurants. Well, he got hit very hard by this virus shutdown. He had to cut way back, lay people off, and change over to carry out food. Well, that's not working out very well. People don't do high end carry out. They order pizza. Olivia is terrified. She has a two-year-old and another on the way, and she depends upon money from her parents. The parents are doing pretty well, but they can't support her and Phillip forever.

"Well, Phil and Olivia were at this political luncheon at this downtown hotel. Marty spotted Phil. You know he's extremely good looking. Well, anyways, while Olivia was talking with a group of women, Marty gets up next to Phil. Gretchen heard the whole thing. This Marty creature asks Phil if he believes in something called the Modern Morality Standard. When Phil asked her what it was, she took his hand and said she'd like to explain it to him, but he'd first need to guess the color of her panties. Well, just like that the two of them took off and got a room.

"Well! The next thing you know, Phil takes up with Marty. He's spending everything he takes out of his restaurants on that whore; and telling Olivia to get more money from her parents. Marty talked Phil into joining this pagan sex cult she started. No, I don't know much about it. It's pretty secretive and you need to become a member. But basically, Phil abandoned his wife and little boy to go with Marty to her sex cult meetings. Now he plants his face into that whore's sex whenever he can afford her. Olivia has become a total mess. She's distraught over this. She's moping and crying all the time. She never was very pretty. And now, with their son and another kid on the way, she's no match for Marty in the sex department. She just needs to tough it out and hope Phil comes to his senses; or else she needs to divorce Phil.

"But, here's the thing. There are many men that have lots more money than Phil has. He's young and starting a family. So, why did Marty pick him? I'll tell you why. It's because she can also be willfully evil, that's why. She had to know that Olivia wasn't very sexy to Phil in her condition, so she took full advantage. Poor Olivia, she is devastated.

"Marty enjoys hurting other women; especially married women. It's like a mission quest for her. I tell you; she's got a mental screw loose about that. She's not going to stop until she drains all of us of

all our money. No, I don't know what we can do about it. I need time to think."

Second female gossip, chiming in:

"Doreen is from back there in Maryland. Her family had a big farm on the Magothy River and they belonged to a country club that reciprocates with ours. Doreen made some phone calls. She learned that when Marty was at the exclusive WEX school, one of the parent mothers wanted Marty barred from all their social events. That mother was the wife of some big public utility company executive, and she had a lot of influence in their club. She was on all the committees and very vocal. Well, this mother, her name was Marge, believed Marty had Jewish blood in her because Marty's hair is so soft and silky, and it has that lustrous brown-black sheen with that splash of red in the front.

"Marge got all the WEX mothers to promise never to let Marty attend any of their weekend events or birthday parties for their daughters. Marty was a full timer at WEX and spent her nights and weekends there. She was alone while her classmates went home to parties and events. Marge effectively got Marty ostracized from the time Marty was five years old.

"Marty struck back at those parents by having sex with their daughters' boyfriends. This taking away behavior began in Marty's junior or senior year. Doreen says Marty began doing sex as a revenge thing. Doreen said this Marge woman had Marty's number spotted from the get go. Marge knew Marty would cause trouble.

"Millie thinks there's a chance Marty will get tired of sex and all this trouble will just go away. Do you think she's right?"

First female gossip, correcting second female gossip, again:

"No, Sharon, Millie is just naive. You know how stupid she is. Marty will never become tired of sex. That simply will not happen.

She's a nymphomaniac. Sex is now a disease addiction for her, like drugs. Mary Lou said so. Mary Lou is smart. She says the addiction just builds and builds and gets stronger and stronger. Haven't you noticed how Marty bats her eyelashes and works her mouth with sexy pouts and smiles? She knows exactly what she's doing, I keep telling you. She always puts on her 'please come and fuck me' look. Why? Her disease demands it, that's why. She constantly craves fresh sex from new partners. That's what Mary Lou says.

"At our Big Game gala, the men swooned all over Marty; remember? They couldn't keep their paws off her. They touched her everywhere, pinched her nipples and rubbed her ass and vagina. She didn't make any effort to stop them. She encouraged them and welcomed all of it. She loved it. She teased them about how good it felt to be pawed and fondled, like that. She even giggled while they did that. She wasn't the least bit ashamed of herself. She laid her head against those men's shoulders while they groped her tits and stimulated her vagina. Normal women don't behave that way in public.

"Absolutely, Sharon, she knew what she was doing. She's had plenty of examples from that mother of hers. You've heard about her. You know who she is. Yes, her! She's that Susan woman that took up with that rich Jew, Marvin Sustack. That's her. Yes, Marty's mother broke her own mother's heart, destroying the dignity of that entire family to sell herself for money like she did. That family was good Catholic stock. They were poor people; but noble. Susan doesn't even go to parish services anymore. She no longer speaks to her aging mother, either. It's very sad. Her craven goings on tarnished that good, descent family.

"How? Come on Sharon, you mean you haven't heard? She services Sustack's big clients! Yes, that's exactly what I mean. He sets them up for her, like he's her pimp but it is all professional and high-class business-like whoring. She rolls in furs, jewels, gold, and money.

She gets chauffeured to work in a Rolls Royce! Yes, I'm talking about Marty's mother, that one. Back when our first depression and the war were going on, while people were in bread lines and begging for food, she was eating caviar and filet mignon; rolling in her furs and diamonds. That was her reward for fucking her ass off with Marvin and the firm's clients.

"Her poor husband died in a car accident. Some say he died on purpose because he couldn't stomach her whoring. I've never seen so many diamonds and rubies as Susan Mallory wears. She's older now; but she still has damn good, drop dead gorgeous, looks. I guess she takes good care of herself and gets cosmetic work done. I hear she still whores. She has several long-term favorites. She was Marvin Sustack's whore right up until the day he died. Yes, she was and she has no shame over what she's all about, either. There's not a single moral fiber in that mother's body; nowhere. She's shameless and she's a little psycho, too, just like her daughter, Marty.

"Gladys and Irene were friends of Susan's since high school. They told me she buys abstract paintings, especially Picasso's and Franz Kline's. Irene said abstract art puts Susan's mind into a different place while she's doing her whore tricks. Irene said Susan has this obsession with Kline, not just as the artist; but also the man. She carries a picture of him in her purse, even pulls it out and looks at it after she does a trick, like she imagines she just did Kline. He was a very handsome, strong football player. Yes, he's dead now.

"And, get this! She obsessed over this Kline guy for years, trying to buy all his art works. She found out his first works were sketches for his high school yearbooks so she bought up all the old yearbook copies. She paid six million dollars for one nineteen thirty-one Gach-tin Bambil, that's the name of that yearbook. She's totally crazy with her obsession over this Kline artist. She thinks that yearbook was the last one that survived the depression and the war. With all those old classmates of Kline's dying off and their kids just tossing the parents'

yearbooks away, Susan just went and bought it. She thinks she now owns every one of them that still exist.

"Why?" Gladys said Irene told her that Susan is extremely possessive, like psycho possessive. She's always been possessive because she never had much as a child. She psychologically sees something in Kline's work that helps her justify being a whore. She likes that feeling and she doesn't want anyone else to have it. She wants to keep the feelings that Kline's work gives her, all to herself.

"Irene said Susan will stare at a Kline for an hour, like it's magical. She lets her mind go into it, sort of; and then her morality does a U turn inside her thoughts and her mind comes back out of that Kline abstract all changed and just peachy fine with her being a totally immoral whore. And, she's insanely in love with her mental images of her and Kline, because Kline's art enables her to do what she needs to do for Sustack. It's like she's obsessed with Kline because he survived the Spanish Flu and came to her across time to sanction her immorality through his art. Somehow Kline's art tells Susan's mind that she's okay and totally normal being a shameless whore.

"Gladys thinks those abstract Kline pieces keep Susan's mind in an okay place. They compartmentalize her mind, sort of; make her feel really good about herself while she does her tricks. They kind of do for Susan what aspirin does for normal people. Not just make her feel okay like aspirin does, mind you, but make her feel really good and enthused about her whoring, like she's being a noble woman to put herself out there like she does.

"I suppose those pieces help Susan overcome her Catholic guilt upbringing and make her mind feel really positive about tricking. Kline's abstracts kind of point out that the world isn't exactly fit together perfectly and that it's okay to think and see things differently. Kline's work has that effect on Susan. She's vicariously fallen in love with that dead artist. It's like she mentally believes every man she's doing becomes Kline himself, somehow.

"How should I know, Sharon? It's like an enabling thing. Kline's abstracts enable Susan to be okay with not having morals and that yearbook enables her to believe Kline is all hers. I told you. She bought up all those yearbooks so no one else can have a Kline; not one single one! She psychologically imagines that Kline is her secret lover, not Marvin or any of her tricks. Do I think she's monogamous? No, she's anything but monogamous. But she's mentally monogamous with Kline. Totally possessive. She must have him. You bet she must. It's a need; a promiscuous dream obsession. I can't explain it. It just is. Who knows how she does that? Well Sharon, we all know when we spread our legs it's actually all about what's happening inside our heads, don't we?

"Does the mother's behavior help you understand the daughter? I'm not so sure. Marty is even more mentally off balance than Susan is. No wonder! Look at the example Susan set for her. The difference is that Marty doesn't need to imagine she's doing some artist when she whores. Marty just loves being a whore, period. She lives to have a cock inside her. She pushes this Modern Morality Standard. It's a pagan sex cult belief system. Everything that's immoral, magically becomes moral; and everything that's moral and normal, somehow becomes immoral. It's all upside down compared to our world. It's like you're climbing up a ladder to go down the Devil's staircase; something like that. Her mind disassociates reality. Her mother's mind, not so much.

"Marty is on a mission to outdo her mother. I'm certain of that. She's got some inner compulsion to break out of an anger cocoon and escape from it, the way a butterfly does. Anyways, some say she has the nympho disease; but whatever she has she certainly has no shame about it. Why, at the gala Marty put herself out there for those men like she was a shameless ally cat. She even wore a dress that made her look like an ally cat!

"And, did you know that Marty did this huge photo spread for a porno magazine? Yes, there were ten full pages of her doing

intercourse with her porn partners in all these different positions, some pages had six photos on a page. I'm surprised you didn't know about it. Well, you know that new doctor and his wife, those two who adopted the two girls from eastern Europe? Their names? I think Lavonna and Lavonia, something like that. It doesn't matter. Listen to me. Gladys told me that, one weekend while their parents were away, those two girls had teenage boys in the house. Oh, they're about fourteen or fifteen and the boys were from fifteen to eighteen. Well, will you just listen?

"Those two girls got their hands on that porno magazine with that ten-page photo layout of Marty fucking and sucking cocks every which way imaginable. And, guess what? Those girls were in their parents' bedroom with those boys and all these kids were practicing doing these porn scenes. Yes! Those two girls were fucking and sucking all those boys; and this went on for two whole days. I guess one of the boy's parents got wind of it. No, there's no police involved, just that the doctor grounded his two girls.

"But can you imagine what this country is coming to? Think about it. Kids are practicing to become porn stars! Porn needs to be made illegal. No exceptions. How will those two girls ever become good Christians after that? The magazine? I don't know. I guess they found it in their parents' bedroom. Well, I know it won't be outlawed; too many people are into it. It's addictive; and it is spreading more every year. Well, look where it's taken Marty. I'll bet she was once a sweet innocent child. I can't imagine how an innocent girl could end up becoming a porn star.

"Ed? Didn't you hear about what he did with her? Oh, Jesus! Why Ed two-fingered her right there in front of everyone. He kissed her sex, too. Shameless? There's a better word for those two, Sharon: 'Depraved!' Yes, that's what they are, depraved! Why? How would I know? They just did that. Yes, Sharon, right there in front of everyone! I said I don't know. She didn't care that people were watching

the two of them. No. Ed just got after her, like he forgot where he was; forgot or didn't care. I suppose her behavior suits Ed perfectly. He's always been mentally off about whores. He has a thing for them. George said he does, that's who; said Ed prefers whores to regular women; said Ed told him whores are the most honest business people he knows.

"What goes on in a man's mind? Hell, Sharon, that's all over the place. Some feel like they're getting away with cheating on their wives; so those men feel guilty about being with her. Others feel it's just good sex; those men are like dogs. They don't put much thought into it. Others are star struck and they fall in love with her. She gets into their minds and they think about her; start caring about her. And they want more of her. They become her regulars.

"Those types lose all their pride and self-respect. They just let her use them all she wants. And they don't care. They don't even care that she has other lovers. When they are with her, all other thoughts fall away from their minds. They experience a rapture state; become kind of like a cat with fresh catnip. They can't leave her alone; can't get enough of her; and nothing else, and nobody else matters to them. They even leave their wives and kids, just to have some time with her. Deep down, they know she's only using them; but they don't even care.

"What about her mind? You've got to be kidding! It's why she lives and what she lives for. She has no soul. No. That's empty. Every man she seduces is a victory for her empty soul. Every sexual experience is nirvana; an ecstasy of reconfirming her self-worth. It's proving to herself that she is desirable and worthy of a man's love.

"She feels that extra special kick when she's having a wonderful time fucking a man; and also ripping the guts out of the woman who loves him. She likes that feeling; lots. She knows she's making another woman feel emptiness, like herself. It's like a blood sport thing. There's a winner and a loser; but in her game of take-away the

loser loses a big chunk of her life. Marty commits psychological mur-
der; tears the other woman down; drags that woman's soul down
into the abyss where she lives. That's the same abyss her mother put
her in, when she abandoned her.

"Mary Lou said that Marty has an empty hole in her heart, and
she's going to keep whoring until she finds a man who can fill it.
With what? Why love, of course. Mary Lou says the woman doesn't
know what love is about; so, she's mentally confused over that; and
then, she gets love mixed up with sex. Mary Lou says Marty can't
recognize the difference between love and sex.

"When? Who knows? When some man finally takes a good hold
of her and loves her for who she really is, I guess. No, I don't know
any man who could find love buried inside a woman like her. She
feels something for some guy named Bob. He works with David Sus-
tack. I heard rumors that Bob and Marty are in love; that they stay
together nights when she's not off somewhere, whoring with another
man.

"She must have honest feelings for her Bob fellow. I think she
loves him. Why? She always goes back to him. Yes, always him. He
must be like a security blanket for her. Maybe he fills some need, or
he connects with her, somehow. I don't know enough about him or
their relationship to explain it. I hear he's a tireless worker. He's all
work, work, work. He's plenty smart, like all those Sustack people.
And he's good-looking. He's tall and muscular; full head of sandy
blond hair; beautiful blue eyes.

"No, I have no idea what he sees in her, besides her looks and
the sex. But they seem connected on some level, somehow. No, he's
not at all like her. She's the only woman he sees. He's the stable one
in their relationship. They must have a weird understanding about
her immorality. He accepts it, somehow. I don't know how he puts
up with her. He must love her unconditionally, no matter how many
men she sees. There must be some kind of deep bond that holds them

together, but I can't imagine what it is. I don't know how he can stand sleeping with her, knowing that she's constantly whoring around.

"Maybe he has no self respect. Maybe he's a pervert and knowing that she's fucking everything in pants helps him get off, somehow. Maybe he has infinite patience for her to work through the issues that make her behave this way. I don't know why he stays with her. That's what I'm telling you. I can't explain it. Love is hard to understand sometimes. Yes Sharon, if they marry, he'll have his hands full for sure. I can't imagine a man living with such a promiscuous, mixed-up mess of a woman. It must be like being with an unbroken, high-spirited mare. She gallops off whenever she sees another stallion; yet she can't stand any stallion paying attention to any other mare besides her."

Second female gossip, deflecting and asserting:

"What Marty needs is a man like that ruffian, Gibby. Oh, come on, you've seen him before. Yes, you know who I mean. Everybody stays wide of him. He'd tame down her whoring ass, real quick. He'd beat some sense into her. Oh, yes, you have, too, seen him, Sharon! Tall, muscled, steely gray eyes, square jawed, big hands; tough and mean, like he's here on loan from hell.

"He's that smelly unshaven mountain man that comes to the Galas, signs on to do guide work, mostly elk and moose, sometimes caribou and grizzly. He never bathes. He STINKS! Yes, that's him, the one who smells so bad he makes me want to throw up. He smokes those wretched cigars; spits his chewing tobacco on the floor; bad teeth, blows his nose in his hands, then wipes that green snot all over his pants; makes those horrible wretched noises with his sinuses that sound like an eighteen-wheeler with a busted gear box. And, he's quick to punch people in the mouth. Don't ever piss him off. He's the vilest, most vulgar, and meanest man there ever was.

"Yeah, that's him. He's disgusting, but he's a great elk guide. My Phil swears by him; says he always finds game because he smells like

a stinky bull elk himself. One that's in rut, rolling in its own piss and mess. Phil says Gibby even smells worse than a rutting herd bull. He was the Marine Corps' finest sharpshooter. He punched out a Captain and got himself discharged. Phil says Gibby can shoot the balls clean off a mouse at a hundred yards. Phil swears he's is a rare, exceptionally gifted, and focused talent. No, he didn't come this year. He was being tried for murder. You didn't hear? Let me tell you.

"*He caught two men poaching his trap lines high up in the San Juan's. They were from someplace on the flatlands. Yep, Gibby caught them messing with his traps. He killed them both at the exact same spot where Al Packer killed and ate those five Democrats in Eighteen Seventy-Three. He shot both those poachers dead. Gibby claimed they drew on him first, so they had it coming. The judge let Gibby off because there were no other witnesses. The facts didn't fit Gibby's testimony. He shot them both four times each: double tapped their guts, military style; and then he shot both of them twice in the head. It looked like Gibby got pissed at them trying to steal his furs, and he wanted them dead.*

"*Nope, neither of them got off a single shot. Yeah, it looked suspicious, like maybe it was cold blooded murder. The sheriff swore Gibby murdered them, but the judge let Gibby go for lack of evidence. Why? Well, in Telluride they don't take kindly to poachers.*

"*And, did you know, that judge is the great, great, great grandson of that old first territorial judge, the judge that gave out the gold stars, whiskey and cigars to those ranchers that hanged the four horse thieves? Yep, the judge they have now is just like his famous ancestor. He even looks like him; same handlebar mustache. He even chews cigars like the old man did. He even throws stuff at people in his courtroom, like the old man did. He'd as soon hang a criminal as jail him.*

"*The territorial hanging judge's old picture still hangs behind the bench in the county courthouse, right behind where the judge sits.*

That picture looks over the judge's shoulder. Nasty, mean looking son of a bitch, he was. That picture stays there as a reminder to his great, great, great grandson that people in those parts don't care for thieves. Besides all that, Gibby and the judge are good friends. They go hunting together.

"Hell no, she wasn't drunk, Sharon. She doesn't need alcohol to get herself itching for sex. Because she's a whore, Sharon! She doesn't need to drink like we do before she does it. She just likes doing it! Yes, she's one of those! Yes, afterwards, Sharon. Sometimes she drinks a Vodka martini with four olives. I don't know. Maybe she feels like a fighter pilot doing a victory roll. No, Sharon. There's nothing innocent about her. She doesn't need to get drunk first because she thinks, in her mind, that her behavior is normal. She thinks we're the abnormal ones. She thinks sex is wonderful, not some obligated, messy business. She's thinks she's saving our men by freeing them from us.

"How? Jesus, don't you understand anything, Sharon? By fucking our husbands until their brains drop out. That's how she thinks she's saving them! She's an immoral, brazen slut, she is. Keep your man close or you could lose him. Some men jump off the deep end over a vagina like hers. Oh, feathers! How did we ever let our guard down?"

"Why? Evelyn's Rusty has a theory on why she is like she is. He says she's got a mental problem that goes back to when Susan left her at that east coast boarding school. He thinks getting abandoned like that gave her a complex, like she came to believe she wasn't good enough for anybody to love her; and so, she gives out sex to get love; but when love does come her way, she has this mental block that keeps her from accepting love. So, she thinks doing the sex act is the end of it and then she needs to move on to her next sex act. Rusty thinks it's all mental with her. If we could break her mental pattern, we might stop her.

"What to do about it? Well, Gretchen and Marge were thinking we should invite her to a tea with biscuits, only put salt peter in her biscuits to cool her down some; and send her salt peter biscuits every day so's she gets used to eating them and she loses her sex drive. It's an anaphrodisiac, Sharon. It's a turn off drug that kills the libido. It has the opposite effect that catnip has on a cat. It keeps people from feeling sexual.

"But Helen and Tina want to use force with her. They want to buy leg chains like those old English kings used on their women to lock their ankles together. They want to be vigilantes. Yes, vagina vigilantes. You heard me right. They're going to follow her and break into her room while she's doing one of our husbands; and then they'll hold her down and put those leg clamps on her and lock the chains onto her clamps so she can't spread her legs anymore, except to walk in little steps; and then they'll throw away the key. They want some of us to join them so we can follow her in shifts, like the detectives follow crooks in the movies. They're looking for volunteers. No, Sharon, they're not crazy. They're serious. For Christ's sake, Sharon, you can't just laugh this off! We need to do SOMETHING!"

The gossips needed a scapegoat to bear the burden for their precarious situation. They focused on Petunia and Fred, opining that their marriage was the weakest link in their social group. They roundly blamed Fred for their misfortune. He allowed himself to be vulnerable to the whore. He opened the door widely for Marty's access to these women's menfolk and their precious wealth! They shunned Fred. They wailed and lamented about the misfortunes of Petunia, his poor wife who moved to Florida to live with her mother; but they also castigated Petunia for not being a more attentive wife.

A cold chill swept through their sensible world. Not only had the vivacious, shameless whore crashed their social circle; she chose to not even stand among them or befriend any of them after her successes. Instead, she remained aloof and apart from them, as if she was an alien, observing them; waiting to devour them. She even contemptuously snubbed them. At their gatherings, they watched her. They noticed that she coolly watched them, like a fearless predator walking nearby; measuring them, alert for a sign of weakness in any one of them; always sizing up their terrified herd.

Marty's boldness unnerved them; drove fissure cracks into their faux confidences. She made no pretenses toward adopting their morals, but remained eager to poach away weak husbands who tipped his interest in her. The social ladies held their collective breaths; silently prayed that their husbands would not betray them; that they would not be the next to suffer Petunia's fate.

Marty had arrived at the gala as Fred's trophy ornament; but she left that evening as the trophy quest of many hunters. In the days that followed the gala, six of the men who had salivated while watching her descend the stairs called U G G A, requesting an in-home appointment visit from Marty. All said they were eager to explore their financial options. Demand for Marty's account servicing skills mushroomed.

After their gala evening, the trophy hunters did not reflect about the new guns they examined or the hunts they booked. They steeped themselves in dreams over what they saw. Their libidos felt more primal, visceral urges than any hunting brochure or animal head had ever stirred. Their worlds became tossed and unsettled. Their manly urges summoned them. They yearned for a new, different kind of hunt. And they fantasized about the promiscuous newcomer.

Marty's vagina became their newest trophy fetish. Being seen with her, opening a car door for her, walking into a charity ball with her, being photographed for the society page with her, became an obsession for several of the club members. Antler sizes and videos of their hunts, suddenly seemed trivial and insignificant. They became passé; silly games for boys. Their guns and exotic hunts had gotten upstaged. Marty was their new, ultimate man-prize.

Fred merely shrugged off the group's social shunning. After all, he was Plaintown's most iconic solitary hunter; acclaimed by all for his steely determination. Nothing ever changed Fred's core sense of self. No risk, hazard, admonition, or wagging tongue ever deterred him from pursuing his quarry. He continued to flaunt his love for Marty, like he proudly showcased his trophy Mouflon. He continued seeing her, playing exciting intimate games with her, exploring the fascinating new world of BDSM with her, shamelessly showing her off at social events, lavishing expensive gifts upon her and defying all competitors to outdo him. Even Ed's rivalry didn't deter Fred or cause him to waiver in the slightest. He knew he was the first man in the club to bag Marty. He knew he always brought down bigger trophies than Ed; and he knew he had much greater perseverance than Ed.

CHAPTER FIVE

Many waters cannot quench love; neither can the floods drown it: If a man would give all the substance of his house (for love), it would utterly be contemned (undervalued) (Song of Solomon)

DREAM VOICES

Before her conquests of Fred and Ed, before her grand entrance at the Game Hunters' Gala would come, and before she became the hottest topic of gossip fare, Marty was still securely in her hideaway cabin with Carl. She smiled in anticipation of her coming days while drifting through her dreams. Carl still slept soundly. She knew she'd enjoy him again in the morning. No anxieties over where she'd next find satisfaction for her nymphomania had yet troubled her thoughts this glorious morning. Her mind turned a calendar page forward to the middle of next week.

Rita had scheduled seven basketball players from out of town. Marty shared a common bond with Rita. They both adored handsome male studs. They both loved the titillating thrills of Rita's orgy fests; and they always prioritized their schedules for those fabulous sex-sating romps. Rita arranged their next orgy in the bridal sweet of a boutique downtown hotel. Marty loved Rita's orgies. Her friend always selected first class accommodations and always scheduled strong, young athletes. Working as a group, Marty's partners matched her insatiable libido. They paid her extremely well before the festivities. And they tipped her even better afterwards; appreciating how Marty put heart and soul into her fornicating and fellatio. Rita vouched to Marty that all seven of the studs she'd scheduled had magnificent cocks, large and able to hold their erections; and with proven stamina:

"Two of them had orgies with you before. They can't stop raving about what a fabulous whore you are. The other five are anxious to meet you. They've seen your films. They'll be in town three more times this year; and they've booked you for all three visits. I promise you: We will have a glorious fun filled night."

Marty imagined herself exhausted from hours of group sex and multiple orgasms:

'I'm already feeling wondrous anticipation. I can't wait to be the object of so many beautiful men. All so strong! They'll be constantly kissing me, feeling me, touching my vagina. They won't take their hands away from stimulating my body for a minute. So many cocks! And all of them staying so hard! I'll be able to fuck until I'm totally out of my mind; crazy. I want this. I want to be on that euphoria plateau. Bless you, Rita! We'll have a blast.

'I remember how I was the last time. I couldn't stop screaming how much I loved it. I was telling them how good they felt, how much I loved being fucked this way, how thrilled I was to have three cocks inside of me, practically non-stop; how beautiful and adored I felt; and how many times I cried out: "OHHHH, Don't stop! Don't stop! Yes! Yes! Yes! Inside me, that's right. Put it inside my vagina now: OH, Yes! That's where it needs to be. That feels soooo Gooood! Yes, Whee, Oooh! YESSSS!! Will you come for me? Are you going to come for me? I want it. Give It to me. Yes! I feel it. I love being fucked this way. Oh, I love it, love it! Oh, push harder, faster. That's it! I want to keep fucking. I'm coming. Yes! I'm coming. Ohhh! Fuck me, fuck me, fuck me! Yes, bring that cock to me. Here, bring it to my lips. I want to suck it. Yes, give it to me. That's it. That's good. Oh, I love this, sooo much!

'I'm coming again! Oh, Here I come! I'll be there soon, Ohhh! I'm coming! This feels so fantastic. Now, I want you to come inside me. Yes, I'm serious. I want you to, please come inside me. Yes, I'm sure. I want to watch your face while you come. Go ahead. I want you to do it. Yes, all of it. That's it. I feel it now. Yes. It feels so warm, so beautiful. I love what you're doing. Oh, you too, yes, come inside me. Yes, that's it. Now, yes! Now, Ohhh! That feels so nice. I love it. I love it! I love how your cum feels inside me. Yes, I totally love what you're doing.'

Marty pined. Her eyelids wanted to close. She tossed, unready for deep sleep. Her emotions were prowling like a wildcat in heat. Her appointment service showed twelve new Premium Member sessions scheduled for the coming week. Her dreamy smile returned. The numbers of qualified men who wanted her continued growing.

'How wonderful! Life is good; so good.' She fingered her vagina while lost in thoughts of her next orgy. Sleep could wait a little longer.

Her premium membership service was doing a great business. One name stood out prominently on her list. She was shocked to see it. He was a handsome young movie star with a huge box office draw. He was eye candy for women, world-wide. Only a year ago photographs of him and his new bride adorned the cover pages of the tabloid magazines. She remembered seeing his handsome face on the grocery store checkout rack.

'I never expected him to call me,' she thought. *'But, why wouldn't he? His wife is just a skinny twig. She's pale and bony. What was he thinking? She looks like a walking dead person. I don't get what he sees in her. She must have had some good lines to catch him. But by now he's heard it all and she's just boring him. Maybe he isn't getting what he first saw in her? Now, maybe he finds her little acts repulsive, like I do?*

'*Maybe my performance in my latest film captivated him? Maybe he wants more of what he saw? He's very handsome. I'm sure he didn't call me, just to talk. He wants to make love with me. I'm anxious to feel his cock inside me. I'm sure I could fall in love with him. Such a beautiful man! Wasting himself on such a pathetic waif of a woman! He'll be an easy take away. This might even lead to something.*

'*I'll make pleasing him my new priority. The next time the paparazzi capture a photo of him, he'll be holding me in his arms; not his wife. I'll wrap my arm around his neck and press my body against him. He'll love me. He'll be kissing me! The photo will show my hand rubbing his cock. I can't wait for our first date.*' Marty recognized two other callers' names. They were professional football players.

'*Savage brutes; probably think they'll thrust and bang me like I'm a side of beef. But I'll tame them,*' she thought. The rest were businessmen. She reminded herself to call her service in the morning to confirm her scheduling.

Her forward thoughts and finger play achieved a small, sweet orgasm. After her warm release, her thoughts returned to Carl. She had him all to herself now. She would enjoy his wonderful cock and tongue for the next three days! She gave a brief thought to Carl's wife:

'*Thank goodness I'm not a wretched psychological mess like Carl's wife is. I'm glad I can keep my head on straight. I can't imagine having a demented mind like hers. Her thinking is so unhealthy and disordered. Her mental imbalance is so obvious! I can't believe she doesn't see it. She'll probably go home tonight and swallow a whole bottle of aspirin, the stupid fool. I'll be making love with her husband while she's lying on the floor, bleeding out. How pathetic can a woman become?*' Marty smiled a contented smile. Her mind switched channels to happy thoughts.

'I'm so thankful I'm mentally well balanced. I love who I am. I'm perfectly happy and adjusted; Mrs. O'Dell told me so. She told me there's absolutely nothing wrong with me. Her therapy has been an immense help. I love fucking my way through life. Mrs. O'Dell says being a whore is the perfect lifestyle choice for me. She assures me I'm making tremendous progress, adjusting to her new Modern Morality Standard. I'm only supposed to do more of what I'm already doing. Thank goodness I found her. I finally have a shrink that understands me,'

Then, Marty fell asleep. She dreamed that Carl's wife was standing before a bathroom mirror, downing a bottle of aspirin. An ambulance came. The paramedics found her lying on the floor. They were too late to save her. Marty's dream channel changed. Now she was talking to Rita. She and Rita were discussing Carl's wife. They couldn't comprehend why she would choose suicide over kissing Marty's vagina. Marty's head gave a small shake. She changed dream channels again. Miss Iniquity found the sleep waves of her host, embraced them as her own and joined them. Then, when she was securely inside Marty's mind, she spoke to her:

'You pleased me greatly today. The way you rid us of Carl's wife pest was beautiful. It was a wonderful thing, a holy act. Bless you. You showed resolve and courage. The way you destroyed her was brilliant. You were glorious. I'm very proud of you. I love you. Put her out of your mind forever. You are innocent of all wrongdoing; only dream beautiful dreams.'

Carl's wife faded from Marty's brain waves like a dim far away light receding into darkness. Then her mind wanted to leave all thoughts of the wife and dream something new. It smothered its thoughts of Carl's wife, like she was a light from a dying candle that finally guttered and went out. Marty stirred in her sleep and smiled a contented smile.

Another dream entered Marty's mind. The voices of Misses Shameless, Promiscuity, and Iniquity all found her brain waves. They floated in Marty's mind like dream angles, twirled together and embraced each other; and then all three voices kissed her waves and coaxed her to dream deeper dreams.

'Oh, *beautiful girl, you are very much loved by us and many others,*' they whispered and echoed in her sleeping mind. '*Many men seek your love. They are anxious for you. They want to please you. They need to receive your love and give their love to you.*'

Marty soon dreamed that an immense black penis appeared before her. Its yearning head tapped gently against her mouth, then teased her by bumping back and forth across her closed lips. She smiled in her dream sleep, admiring the cock's aspiring hardness and splendid beauty. It spoke to her in its secret silent language of intimacy. It told her it came to see her because it wanted to make her happy, and it wanted to be kissed by her.

Marty's dream state became her comfort zone's psychological companion; her normal world, the one she was accustomed to living in. She spoke softly, telling the cock she loved it and assuring it that she wanted it to be happy, too. Then, she opened her mouth and kissed its head. She told it how beautiful it was and how she loved kissing it. She lovingly stroked the underside of the cock's head with her adoring tongue.

The cock strained mightily and spoke silently to her. It promised her it would become one with her. It said it would love her forever. Marty's dreaming brain waves became aroused. Her mind anticipated the cock's ejaculation. She imagined the opening stanzas of the *Gloria* as the cock began spurting its voluminous stream of semen onto her tongue. As she swallowed it's cum, another gorgeous black cock appeared before her and tapped at her mouth, also anxious for her kisses. Soon her dream became a continuous blur as cock after cock sought her mouth. She kissed every cock's head. Her lips performed felatio strokes over every shaft; and her tongue lavished its teases on every cock's underside and head. Her mouth made delicious erotic love with all of them. Her dream made her moist inside.

She smiled her contentment smile. Her dream mind looked down over her body. Beautiful black men were taking their turns shooting cum into her vagina and onto her nipples and rubbing their grateful loving cocks over her nipples and stomach. They were giving her their love. The *Gloria* sounded its strains over and over, playing adoration of her whoring as affirming accompaniment to her brain waves. Dozens of cocks surrounded her now. Her mind savored the reverence the men were showing towards her. They kissed her everywhere; and they praised her as their goddess.

One by one, in her mind's dream, she French kissed every orgy partner. She was returning love now. Each man, in turns, held her lovingly in his arms. She ran her hands over their muscular arms and backs and asses as she pressed her body close to each of theirs. They took turns kissing her vagina and loving her; then bringing their smiling faces to her mouth and kissing her mouth. She made love with each man in her missionary position and pulled each cock, now magically hard again, deeply inside her. Each lover whispered to her, telling her how much he adored her and loved her, while his shaft performed its loving strokes. Our dream girl smiled. This was her perfect nympho world, where love's pleasures never ended.

Her spirit voices kissed her cheeks and forehead throughout her dream orgy. Little Cupid angels told her she was beautiful in her pleasure quest. Her head rolled slightly toward Carl as she slept. Her dreams were immersed in pleasure, no longer disturbed by memories of Carl's pest wife. Her thoughts were again comported with her nymphomaniac obsessions and compulsions.

Her mind was relaxed and untroubled, completely settled in the rightness of her whoring. She was in the resting state she preferred for her mind. She smiled a contented dream smile and slept soundly. As the first pale light of the morning's sky touched the rooftop of the cabin, she had yet another dream. This time, her mind's channel switched to her present interest: Carl.

She dreamed she had already freshened herself before Carl awakened. She lavished KY jelly inside her vagina to make herself extra juicy for him. She dreamed she was teasing him as he awoke, claiming him as her rightful prize, fairly won by the insightful genius of her perfect murder, and irresistible whoring. She fondled his balls, telling him what a wonderful lover he was. She French kissed him, longingly, while her hand awakened his cock and gradually stiffened it. She then put his balls into her mouth and played her tongue over them. Then she sucked his cock to full hardness and straddled it. She dreamed she was wide awake and whispering to him:

"Hold me close, Carl, and make love with me. I love you and I want you inside me. Help me forget that nasty woman. OH, YES! FUCK ME BABY. FUCK ME HARD!" she commanded him. She then arched her back, presenting Carl with her up-lilted naked breasts and protruding button-bud nipples.

In her dream mind her music played the *Gloria* again. She smiled a wide inviting smile at Carl; and, taking his hands, placed them upon her breasts, urging him to feel her love of life. He gently pinched and squeezed her hard nipples while lovingly massaging her breasts. That sent tremble tingles of hot lust surging through her entire body. She felt the tingles stimulate her in her sleep, as if she were already awake. She dreamed Carl was kissing her nipples and titillating them with his loving tongue. Her sex moistened until it became saturated with her wetness.

She dreamed Carl's stimulation had awakened her pelvis. She was soon, slowly, rhythmically rocking her ravenous vagina over Carl's magnificent cock. She moaned with desire. She inserted his cock into her vagina. She wanted it there. Even in her dream state she knew this cock was Carl's. It knew her and her intimate ways, like no other lover could know her. She dreamed she was taking his cock inside her, slowly, lovingly; the way she loved to make love with him, most times. Her dream thoughts were about the coming waking moments with her lover. She'd kiss him and hug him tightly. She'd be one with him.

Marty would start Carl's day off fresh. She'd make sure he only had her on his mind, by loving him passionately before breakfast. This coming cozy morning, with a fire crackling in the fireplace, she would be her uninhibited best; at the top of her game. She willed herself to be the most loving, most innocently appearing, shamelessly proud, murderous whore any man had ever held in his arms.

She would have slept soundly the night before; and she'd have dreamed of awakening to a victory celebration. Her mind had already imagined their morning. Gloria's anxious vaginal lip petals would engulf the tip of Carl's huge magnificent cock, entice it to a full hard erection. Then her slippery walls would slide its shaft deeply into its home. His cock would belong only to her from then on. She'd hold it within her inner walls. She'd squeeze it and tease it by contracting and releasing it until it was straining wildly with unbridled lust for her. All this while she'd knead his balls until he could no longer hold back his massive ejaculation. Sunrise couldn't come soon enough.

That next morning the sun's wakening rays peeked through the cabin's curtained windows. Marty's mouth and tongue played happily with Carl's penis in the filtered light of their new dawn. She felt glorious and in control of everything in her world.

"Do you like the ways I kiss your cock, baby?" She whispered to him. Carl groaned. He was awakening into Marty's eternal nympho world. She was in her awakened comfort zone, performing felatio. Her last night's dream had become her morning's reality.

"You get really sensitive when I suck you like this, don't you?" She lifted her head from his cock and looked into Carl's eyes. *"You know I love kissing your cock's head and how much I love running my tongue over it, don't you?"*

Carl could only sigh at the pleasures Marty was giving him.

"Oh, our friend is really big and hard now. He's anxious to come inside me now, isn't he? Is the big dog ready to come inside me now?" Marty had moved her head down to Carl's lower abdomen. Her face lay next to his cock. She kissed its shaft with her lips, giving it her signal that she was eager to entertain it. She then spoke to Carl's cock, as if it was a real person, with its own vocal skills.

"Do you want to come inside my vagina and get out of the cold, you sweet, wonderful man? Are you ready to play inside me? Would you like to play inside me, where it's nice and slippery and warm? Oh, of course you would! Come on, let's have fun! Let's play inside Marty's vagina, where it's nice and warm."

Carl could only smile and nod as Marty used her hand to guide Carl's cock into her waiting vagina. She slowly lowered herself onto Carl's trusting member while placing his hands upon her breasts. She stimulated herself with two fingers of her hand while she began sliding her vagina in a gentle, twerking, rocking motion upon Carl's cock. Countless times this method had brought Carl and Marty to beautiful simultaneous orgasms and there was every reason to believe that would happen for them again, this morning.

Marty experienced rapture that morning. While her physical libido was being sated, her inner voices cheered her. Their spirits soared. They skipped and danced joyfully over an imaginary, endless green meadow; happily congratulating each other over how well they had each played their voice roles; helping Marty destroy her nemesis. They frolicked and laughed joyfully. They romped and sang: *'His wife is gone!'* and they rolled upon their imaginary grass, savoring their same delightful sensations of lust and conquest that Marty herself felt, while making love with Carl. And also believing, as Marty did, that their adversary had gone home last night, downed a bottle of aspirin and bled to death.

After a few moments, Carl's penis spurted its raging hot stream of semen over Marty's highly sensitized clitoris. Then, driven by his powerful thrusts, his massive, still shooting cock completed its total immersion plunge. Marty fully expected Carl to do this. It was his signature move after his copulation climax. He held himself deeply inside her. He loved these long immersions in her unrepentant, iniquitous vagina. The two of them had their oneness now, united by their mutual passion lusts; just the two of them; no wife to bother them; never again! Marty's legs pulled Carl's cock tightly into her, holding him ever closer to her while she cradled and rocked his body. And she French kissed him with heartfelt passion.

While Marty secured her prize and coaxed every last measure of semen from him, miles away two passers-by noticed the deadly carnage wrought by her determined ruthlessness. A car, driven by Carl's wife, lay mangled, burned, and crushed in the middle of a boulder field a thousand feet below the highway. The car's driver was obviously dead.

Marty French kissed Carl long, passionately; and then playfully, after he finished ejaculating that morning. She always engaged in after-play as part of her tradecraft. But this morning her playfulness was subtly different. She conveyed with it a special meaning; a profound importance to every kiss and touch which she gave him. She was immensely proud of him; and feeling very much in love with him. She nuzzled her body close to his and slowly rubbed his massive chest:

"I love playing with your chest after we make love, Carl," she purred.

She kissed his nose and eyes and forehead while her hand played with his chest and stomach. She knew her tradecraft well. She was securely confident that only she would *ever* know the details of the deathly interaction she'd had with Carl's wife the night before. She was certain Carl's wife would never inconvenience her love making again. Carl was all hers now; for as long as she wanted him. That was all that mattered to her. This morning's tryst had proven to her that the end, indeed, had justified the means.

"Tell me how you feel about me, Baby. I need to know you love me. I need to hear you tell me. I need to feel that you really love me," she whispered as her doe eyes and earnest loving smile searched Carl's face. She sought affirmation of her love making; and through that affirmation she believed she would receive his understanding acquiescence and unspoken approval of her murder.

Her hand moved lower until it gently stroked his cock. She pressed her naked body to his and soulfully kissed his mouth, shamelessly applying more of her tradecraft. His eyes were closed. He was smiling. She recognized that Carl had entered an entranced-like state of sublime adoration, thinking only of her and their love making. In Carl's state of mind, even if he intuited what she'd done to his wife, she had no doubt he would neverthe-less accept what she did. She knew he wished to be rid of her. Her intuition told her he would love her even more for making that happen.

Her confidence in Carl's love for her was absolute. She was positive it was stronger than any misgivings that might arise if he ever learned she was a serial murderess. She had dispatched the wife; and now she had Carl where she wanted him. Her victory was complete. She wanted Carl to have her and ravage her when-ever he desired her. She wanted to have that special inner feeling that she was the world's most incorrigible, shameless, murderous whore and that she held within her a special secret that she had taken Carl's wife from him, forever.

That gave her lovemaking a special, endearing twist that made Carl ever dearest to her heart. She knew she would always love him; always joyfully give herself to him; always cherish the breathtaking, spectacular initial penetrations of his magnificent cock. Now, all she needed to hear was his affirmation. Most certainly, he would voice his love and approval of her and everything she did. What else *could* he say? She awaited his response to her command. Knowing that, surely, she had done something nefarious, possibly heinous, to his wife, would he nevertheless confess his love? Did he love her? She waited to hear him say it:

"Marty, of course I LOVE you. I deeply love everything about you and everything you do. I'll always love you. I'll love you no matter what you've ever done or what you ever will do. I love you. I totally love you." he smiled warmly as he squeezed her body tightly against his and kissed her. Carl's penis was hard once more. He was in a rapture state; and anxious to again slake Marty's nymphomaniac disorder.

More to come.

What is it about Marty' condition that enables her to have sincere, loving involvements with multiple partners? Successful Carl offers up his life on a silver platter to her, but sharing her life with Carl is not what Marty wants. Something else is causing our butterfly to flutter. Now, the town gossips are wagging their tongues over Marty's affairs with Fred and Ed. In addition to her two new admirers, Marty's movie career is taking off and her Premium Memberships are increasing fast. Her Nymphomania has enabled Marty to manage both her career and her lovers, thus far.

As fortune would have it, our butterfly is about to meet Bertie and George, a successful couple who believe, after their terrible misfortune, that Marty is exactly what they think they need. The Spirits play their role in our next fateful matching. During film studies sessions we'll hear Marty, Bertie and George discuss erotic production techniques, and we'll discover what causes Marty's intense fascination with Marshawn, a favorite performing partner. We can listen in, while Marty reveals her latest trysts to David. Listen carefully and decide. Will Marty reveal more than she should?

I'm Melanie Monarch, your audio book narrator. Come flutter along with me as I narrate BUTTERFLLY CONFIDES, the fourth book of THE SECRET BUTTERFLY (tm) SERIES.

www.ingramcontent.com/pod-product-compliance
Lightning Source LLC
Chambersburg PA
CBHW040530170726
48295CB00012B/402